# HIS LOVELY DISGRACEFUL DAUGHTER

## The endless 'Summer of Love'

*Bliss was it in that dawn to be alive;*

*But to be young was very heaven!*

– Meg Denby, quoting William Wordsworth

In memory of
# Roderick Thomson
ITURI PUBLICATIONS, 1999-2013

Also from Martin Horrocks and Ituri

*Girl at the Top Table*

# HIS LORDSHIP'S DISGRACEFUL DAUGHTER

Martin Horrocks

PLUS END-NOTES ABOUT THE 1960s

Ituri
www.ituri.co.uk

**His Lordship's Disgraceful Daughter** is published by

**Ituri Publications**

www.ituri.co.uk

ISBN 9780992965808

© Martin Horrocks, 2014

The moral rights of the author have been asserted
A CIP record for this book is available from the British Library

**The characters and events depicted in this novel are fictitious. No resemblance is intended to actual persons or to real events other than those that provide the period context.**

Cover design by Book Production Services, London:
**www.bookproductionservices.co.uk**

Front cover picture © iStockphoto.com/CareyHope
Back cover picture © iStockphoto.com/Druvo

Set in 10pt on 13pt Century Schoolbook with titles in Helvetica by Book Production Services

Printed and bound in the UK by 4edge Ltd
www.4edge.co.uk

**All rights reserved. This publication or any section of it may not be reproduced, stored in a retrieval system, or transmitted in any form or by any means (electronic, mechanical, photocopying, recording or otherwise) without the prior written permission of the publisher**

*ASTERISKS IN THE TEXT INDICATE ENTRIES IN THE END-NOTES BEGINNING ON P126*

# ONE

NO ONE spotted Meg at Heathrow Airport. When a film star looks like everyone else, it's a safe bet she can move around undisturbed. Meg Denby was the fantasy girl next door Sixties-style – the scorcher that no one ever quite lives next door to. And Meg's own home, Lowmere Abbey, had no next door, sitting alone in 4,000 good Yorkshire acres.

Gossip column coverage of Lord and Lady Chilcott's only daughter had done Meg no harm in her film career. She had already starred in three feature films, and was finishing her fourth. She was 24, gorgeous, five foot eight with cascades of long black hair, which from time to time she cleared away from her face with a characteristic backwards flick of the head. THE GIRL WHO HAS EVERYTHING, as the Daily Mirror described her.

Except that right now she didn't have Everard Hughes. Meg's actor lover was late in leaving the customs hall. She spotted other passengers from the LA flight from the tags on their luggage. Perhaps he was signing autographs for the customs officers – or 'my son' or 'my daughter'. Everard never missed a chance like that.

Finally he emerged from the customs area, walking with the natural swagger that lean, six foot two and the prime of life – he was 27 – produces. He was tanned from three months in the California sun, his blond hair almost as long as Meg's. Smilingly refusing autograph hunters in his path, he flung his arms wide in a theatrical gesture and allowed Meg to collapse into his arms.

'It's been too long,' she murmured as she nuzzled his chin on which his overnight stubble could be felt.

'And a damned long, tiring flight,' he responded prosaically.

It would take more than a touch of travel weariness to dampen Meg's sunny mood. After the long months of separation she had Everard back, her Everard, the father of her child. She knew little more of what he'd been doing in Hollywood than she read in the film magazines and occasional gossip paragraph in the newspapers. He was not the best of letter writers, and phone calls could be awkward and of poor quality.

'I want to hear everything about everything in Tinseltown,' she said lightly as they drove back to the flat in Meg's Austin Healey 3000 *.

'And so you shall, when we're back home,' he said, volunteering nothing.

'Sweetheart, surely it's time you dumped the Healey,' he added. 'It's last year's game if not the year before's.' Everard Hughes had returned from Hollywood with his obsession with appearances reinforced. 'Darling, appearances are what we strolling players are about,' he would intone frequently.

Meg, at the wheel, reached across and rubbed his trousers. She felt him hardening under the thin American fabric, but he pushed her away as she tried the zip.

'Ev, darling, what's the matter?' she asked. 'You've been a grump since we met.'

'I haven't, and nothing's the matter. I'm tired and jet-lagged, that's all.' Evidently it didn't sound convincing

---

* HERE AND THROUGHOUT THE BOOK, AN ASTERISK INDICATES AN ITEM IN THE END-NOTES BEGINNING ON P126

even to him. 'Anyway, I mustn't get too excited now if I want to ... later ...' He let the thought die away.

The rest of the journey to the flat in Bloomsbury was made with not especially comfortable small talk from each of them. Meg was aware that Everard hadn't asked about their son, Benjamin, now one year old – surely one of the first things that a father is supposed to do after a long spell abroad. When Meg brought up the subject, Everard managed the polite interest of an uncle or a cousin.

When the front door of the flat was closed, Meg couldn't wait to undress him. She took his trousers down first; then the shirt. She pulled off his shoes and socks, and finally removed his underpants. She sensed that Everard was on auto-pilot as he in turn took off her T-shirt, bra and micro-miniskirt *. He seemed to have forgotten about her shoes so she slipped them off herself.

They were still in the hall and, not noticing the cold, she lay down on the lino. She was soaking even before he pulled off her panties. He entered her immediately. Meg shuddered as she felt him go in deep and hard. That was Ev all over, Ev the swordsman – he delivered just about anywhere, anytime, whatever his mood. One moment she was complaining about his grouchiness, and the next moment he had her on fire. She climaxed quickly, and a few seconds later so did he.

'God, I'm tired,' he said. It was five minutes since they had reached the flat, and they were the first words he'd said. He went into the bedroom and fell asleep.

The next morning, Meg said they should go to see Benjamin in Yorkshire. The child lived with Meg's parents – because of her work commitments, it was said. He was being brought up by Lady Chilcott, or more precisely by a resident nanny with cook taking a turn on nanny's day off.

'It's a beautiful day for a run,' Meg said brightly. 'Let's get going straightaway.'

Everard, munching toast, seemed not to hear. 'You don't get marmalade like this in California,' he remarked.

All evening and half the night Meg had been trying to jolly him out of his mood of indifference. Now she flared up; she couldn't help herself.

'Fuck it, Everard, who gives a fuck about marmalade? This is your son we're talking about.'

'And yours,' he incautiously responded.

'Oh fuck off, Everard! Don't you want to see Ben at all?'

'Calm down, sweetheart. Of course I do. I'm desperate to see him. But I've got a living to earn, remember. I must see Ken urgently [Ken was the agent for both of them]. I've had welcome home messages from several of the gang. I must say hallo to them. And the *Evening Standard* want to do another profile of me – remember their article last year? I thought I might fit that in before we head for the wild north.'

'Well that's bloody it,' Meg shrieked. 'With you, it's always about *me*. Me, me, me. Never mind our son. And while we're on the subject, don't I have a living to earn as well?'

It crossed his mind to say that with a substantial trust fund income and indulgent parents, actually no. Fortunately he didn't.

All this time they had been glaring at each other across the kitchen table. Now he got up and moved towards her, intent on embracing her to kiss it better, and the rest. But she backed away so he got nowhere near.

'Darling, what's this all about?' he persevered. 'All I'm saying is that we'll go tomorrow.'

'Wrong,' she replied. 'Perhaps you're going tomorrow. I'm going now.' With that, she flung herself into the bedroom and started to pack a bag.

Meg's anger continued to grip her as the Healey nosed its way through the North London suburbs and on to the recently completed M1 motorway *. The fine sunny day and the reassuring thrum of the engine gradually lightened her mood. The wind whipped through her hair as the car devoured the open road at an easy eighty. By the time she passed the sign for Northampton she was replaying the events of the last few hours quite calmly. By Rotherham she had begun to question herself. Poor Ev … had he been so unreasonable in wanting to catch up with his pals? Had she been an utter bitch? Would an extra 24 hours before he saw Ben have made any difference?

She left the motorway at Leeds for the short journey to Ripon. As she drove through the picturesque town – or rather, city by virtue of its cathedral – she desperately wanted to make it up with Everard. She must phone him as soon as she could. Spotting a phone box, Meg pulled up. The box stank and was full of litter. But this had to be done, she told herself. One of the coins jammed in the slot. That was it then. A reverse charge call through the operator would not be the best way to start a peace parley. Another box farther along the road was in an equally disgusting state, but it worked.

Everard seemed to be out because her own voice inviting her to leave a message came back to her from the answering machine. Did he know how to retrieve messages? New technology * and Everard didn't go together. Or perhaps he would be in the flat not knowing how to override the answer mode, in which case he would hear her but couldn't speak.

'Ev darling, just a silly spatiwat,' she said. 'Of course you should see Ken and the gang. Ben will be ready for you tomorrow. I was being sillikins. I'm almost at Lowmere. Give me a ring. Missing you dreadfully already, lovely boy.'

He hadn't cut in on the message. She blew him ten kisses, and hung up.

# TWO

LOWMERE ABBEY was its usual comforting self. A long building of three storeys, it was built of severe, grey Yorkshire stone, but still managed to seem more like a home than a barracks. The chancel of the old monastic church had been incorporated into the house at one end, and formed the family's private chapel. It was the only remaining part of the abbey from which Lowmere took its name. The rest had been taken down stone by stone with many of them used in the present house.

Invisible from any public road, the mansion was surrounded by carefully devised parkland with sweeping lawns to the front and rear. To one side were the stables and outbuildings; on the other side was the Victorian legacy of a magnificent herbaceous border. Meg's mother, Lady Chilcott, took a very personal interest in the border.

As she brought the Healey up the drive, Meg knew she would find her parents at tea. Lord and Lady Chilcott were far from being retired from the world – her father had been a government minister not long before, and was still active in the House of Lords – but they had created an ambience at Lowmere where it seemed to be 'always afternoon'. It was a world that Meg could hardly wait to leave – but which pulled her back again and again.

After quickly greeting her mother and father, she rushed to the nursery to see her son. This had been her nursery, too. She remembered it from the days of postwar austerity. It was cleaner and brighter now, with a smart, well equipped bed-sitter next door for the resident nanny.

This girl, an Italian called Julia, was on the floor with Ben playing with bricks. Having unsteadily built a tower of three bricks and seeing it topple over, the boy wanted to return to the task. Anger could be seen on his 12-month-old face as his mother took him into his arms and kissed and cuddled him.

Eventually Meg put him down. Ben seemed distressed. 'Mamma,' he said, looking straight at Julia. Montmorency, a shabby cat of mixed parentage, chose that moment to jump into the nursery through an open window. Ben's attention was immediately engaged. 'Gatto,' he said.

'Was that Italian?' Meg asked incredulously, hoping she had misheard.

'I didn't quite hear it,' Julia replied uneasily.

'Those words sounded like Italian to me. Surely you don't speak to Ben in Italian?'

'Not usually,' the girl answered, looking even more uneasy.

'Look, Julia, you do not speak to my son in Italian – ever. Have you got that? I don't want Ben getting confused as he learns to talk.'

'All right,' said Julia. But Meg knew that the maternally minded Julia wouldn't stop and there was nothing that she, Meg, could do about it short of getting the nanny sacked or taking care of Ben herself.

Throughout the evening Meg was on edge waiting for Everard's call. She rang several of their circle – her former flatmate Lucy Plessey, the film director Tommy

Radicek and even the writer Arnold Haverstock, with whom Meg had had a long, live-in affair starting when she was a luscious 18-year-old – but no one knew where he was. It was hopeless. She phoned the flat a couple more times and left messages, summoning her acting powers to try to avoid sounding desperate. Still no word.

She went to bed early. Even the thought of Ben above her, sleeping peacefully next to Julia, didn't help her to a good night's rest.

The next morning Everard still didn't phone. Meg became increasingly anxious. He turned up before lunch, acting as if nothing had happened. She didn't dare ask him where he had been or why he hadn't rung for fear of provoking another row.

In bed after lunch he was especially tender. 'It's so good to be home,' he murmured. Having wrapped himself around her, he was tracing the bumps of her spine with an index finger.

'Ooh, do that again!' said Meg as he reached the small of her back. She could lie like this forever, the feeling was so delicious. This was the Ev she was in love with – gentle, caring, yet passionate. She had only to see his bare chest to become aroused. Now, however, she wanted nothing more than to linger in his arms.

'I'll do it again and again and again, my lady!' he responded, his voice louder with excitement. 'So I've discovered a new erogenous zone, have I?'

The words 'erogenous zone' seemed to fly along the corridor and down the staircase to the great hall, where Lord and Lady Chilcott were preparing to open the house for the day's paying visitors.

'Shush!' she said. 'My parents will hear.'

'Meg Denby, where on earth did you come by these

middle-class values?' he joked. 'Why shouldn't your parents know you're having sex while they are fiddling with their account books?'

She giggled at that. 'There's something so wicked somehow in going to bed in the afternoon,' she managed.

In reply Everard uncoiled himself and pushed Meg on to her back. He was obviously going to do it again. She had been content to lie wordlessly in his arms; she was equally content with this. Everything was all right this afternoon.

Later, they walked hand-in-hand in the gardens, giving visitors a wide berth. It became a game. 'Visitor ahoy!' Meg would cry, pulling Everard behind a bush or back to front so they wouldn't be recognised. He allowed himself to be pulled, but he didn't share her dislike of being seen.

The pond was far enough away from the house that the visitors rarely reached there. It was an enormous pond, and if it had been shown on the map as a lake would have been a popular attraction. This afternoon no one was at the pond.

Meg pointed to the naked lady statuette in the centre of the pond. 'When we were children we used to skim stones at that,' she said. 'Not throw ... that would be too easy. The idea was not just to hit it but to hit it in as few bounces as you could.

'It's 18$^{th}$ century and terribly valuable. Daddy was furious when he found out what we were doing. We had to promise not to do it any more – and of course we did. Both my brothers were great skimmers – Thomas was better than Jeremy – and I was pretty good too.'

'Clever girl,' said Everard. 'Show me.'

Meg chose a flattish stone. With a deft sideways flick

of her right arm, she sent the stone to its target in three bounces. 'It's like riding a bicycle,' she said happily. 'Once you know how to do it you never forget. Now your turn.'

'I can't skim,' he admitted.

'Can't skim! Everybody can skim.'

'No. Our garden wasn't big enough to have a pond, and a fierce park keeper always stopped us when we did it in the park.' It was one of the few times when he referred to his modest upbringing in Sunderland.

His father was a bus driver and his mother a clerical assistant in a solicitor's office. A doted upon only child, Everard – born Edward Hughes and always called Eddie – had striking good looks from babyhood. He was good at sports and clever too – clever enough to win a free place at Eton. He then found himself at the country's leading drama school, RADA *. All that marred this seemingly perfect concatenation of qualities was his self-obsession. At the boarding school his broad provincial accent as well as his narcissism let him in for a lot of ragging. He soon lost his accent (but not his self-obsession).

Meg was trying unsuccessfully to pull Everard to the edge of the pond. 'Have a go!' she said. He continued to resist. 'Spoilsport! Then I'll race you back to the house.'

He accepted this challenge, but three months in the Hollywood fleshpots had done nothing for his fitness. Meg had the better speed. After she turned a corner to run along the flower border, he was nowhere to be seen. She slowed herself to a walk. Several visitors stared at her. She could read their thoughts: Is it or isn't it? Yes, it must be! After all, 'family home of the film star Meg Denby' was one of the unofficial attractions of Lowmere Abbey.

And still no Everard. She retraced her steps to find him surrounded by a knot of admirers, signing autographs. He was using the special pen that travelled everywhere with him. Even on a summer weekend in the country he took that pen.

They were at dinner in Lowmere's spacious dining room with its Robert Adam plasterwork and centuries of family portraits sitting comfortably on the panelled walls. The room was at once both huge and intimate. Four of them – Everard, Meg and Meg's parents –filled it well enough.

Lord and Lady Chilcott were both determined to keep the house in use as it was intended. Not for them a flat in one of the wings while the main rooms were abandoned to the visitors.

Lord Chilcott grumbled at the heating bills that this policy entailed, and as a reflection of the straitened times just one maid waited at table. The trusted Beryl stood discreetly at the back of the room next to the serving table, ready to provide food, remove empty plates, circulate with the wine and so on. She never passed on what she learnt about family arguments.

One such started now. Lord Chilcott remarked on the celebrations for the first humans to land on the moon, which had taken place the month before.

'It's a scandal the Americans don't spend those millions on helping their blacks in the inner cities,' said Meg '... To say nothing of the millions they pour into the war in Vietnam.'

'Then say nothing,' said Lord Chilcott, who had heard his daughter on Vietnam too many times.

When Meg referred to a planned peace demo in London, her father recognised the danger signal but couldn't help himself.

'They're wasting their time,' he said. 'Grosvenor Square * last year didn't change anything. They made their point, and the sensible thing is to leave it at that.'

'Is that your idea of democracy, Daddy?' Meg responded. 'Young people can protest their heads off so long as it doesn't change anything!'

'I'm sure the government has taken note of how young people feel, darling,' Lady Chilcott ventured.

'Fat chance!' Meg shot back. 'This is a colonial war by the Americans. Our government should be opposing it, not supporting it.'

Her parents had heard this sort of talk from Meg many times before.

'Darling, I don't think you really mean that,' said Lady Chilcott. 'I think you get it from that dreadful man, Arnold Haverstock.'

'Meg, you know very well that it's nothing to do with colonialism. It's a war to stop communism spreading all over South East Asia,' said Lord Chilcott. 'Obviously we should support that. And incidentally, we should be glad that the Americans have put their hands to it and we haven't had to risk British lives * on the ground.'

'So a wicked policy is all right so long as it doesn't risk British lives, is that it?' said Meg. 'Is that a typical line as practised in government?' (This was a reference to Lord Chilcott's time as a minister.)

All this time Everard was taking an extreme interest in the Brussels sprouts on his plate. 'Were these sprouts grown on the estate?' he asked. Everyone ignored him including Lady Chilcott, who said: 'Meg darling, I don't think you should speak to your father like that.'

'I'm sorry, Mummy, but the war is wicked. What

about the carpet bombing of defenceless villagers from B52s *?'

Lord Chilcott decided that enough was enough. 'Let's agree to differ ...'

'It's not even the North Vietnamese fighters who suffer. They're safe in their tunnels. It's the ordinary peasants who have nowhere to go,' Meg pursued.

'We've heard all this before,' said Lord Chilcott.

'And the use of Agent Orange * to destroy crops so the villagers starve ...'

'It's good that you're concerned about all who suffer, but these are things we can't change,' said Lady Chilcott.

'We can change things if enough of us stand firm!' Meg was almost shouting. 'I'm jolly well going to the demo, and not only that – I'll be speaking.'

'Is that wise?' asked Lady Chilcott.

'Why is it not wise? If they arrest me, they can arrest Vanessa and Jane too' (referring to the actresses Vanessa Redgrave and Jane Fonda, both radical campaigners).

Everard by now had exhausted the interest of the Brussels sprouts and had moved on to the carrots and potatoes. 'Are you going back to Hollywood or are you done for now?' Lord Chilcott asked him.

The star was only too happy to talk at length about his plans and prospects. While no one seemed to be paying much attention, at least the vexed subject of Vietnam had been closed down.

# THREE

VIETNAM was a long way away over the next several days at Lowmere. The only pressing issue was what enjoyable activity to do next. Meg awoke each morning to the prospect of another spacious, eventful day. She didn't know what the events would be, but she knew they would be nice. That was the joy of it.

They lost themselves in the music of The Who, Jimi Hendrix and Crosby, Stills, Nash and Young even as those artists were performing at Woodstock. Hundreds of thousands attended what was hailed as the world's biggest music festival. Exuberant radio reporters spoke of up to four hundred thousand expected to attend. And soon after that would be Britain's turn: the Isle of Wight festival.

'Ev, we must, must go,' said Meg. 'Bob Dylan will be appearing. All we need is a car and a tent, and we're there!'

'Darling, I'd love to but I don't expect to be here,' Everard replied.

He was awaiting the call back to Hollywood for retakes. Meg was between pictures. Ken the agent had sent her two scripts to consider. She accepted both.

Meg was happy. She believed she knew all Everard's weak points, but she loved him just the same. He was impossibly vain. He wasn't interested in books or politics – both were her preoccupations – only in himself. Nor did he care for children, even though one was his own. Of course, he was a stallion and he had bum and biceps to die for. But there was more to him than that. He could be very loving. When he forgot to take himself seriously, he was good company.

She awoke early one morning. Everard's side of the bed was empty. (When Ben came along the polite country house fiction of separate bedrooms had been abandoned with nothing said. They had simply arrived at Lowmere on one occasion to find one bedroom made up instead of two.) Then he appeared bearing a tray with two mugs of tea.

'No need to wait for the maid. I cooked it myself. I'm not just a pretty face,' he said.

'I never said you're a pretty face,' said Meg.

'Then you don't get any tea.'

'You're a pretty face.'

They went riding across the Lowmere fields, with Meg proving herself more accomplished than Everard. 'There aren't many cross-country trails in Sunderland,' Everard pointed out. They went for spins through the wild Yorkshire moors, alternating her Austin Healey with the Jensen Interceptor * that he had brought up from London.

They were not troubled by fans and autograph hunters. Around Lowmere they were well used to Meg. She was just the girl from the big house. As for Everard, he was her boyfriend and some bloke who did acting in London. Farther afield, he was often recognised, but most people were too polite, or too scared, to do anything about it.

In Ripon a girl of about 16 came up to them and said: 'Excuse me, aren't you Everard Hughes?'

Everard agreed that he was. Having hit her bull's-eye the girl was unable to follow it up. She stared and said nothing.

'Are you a visitor in Ripon?' Meg asked to cover the awkward silence.

The girl turned and seemed to see Meg for the first time. 'You're Meg Denby, aren't you? I saw you in *All in a Day's Work*. You're gorgeous. How do you manage to stay so young?'

'That's because I am young,' Meg replied. The girl looked doubtful. 'Just joking,' Meg added. 'Cold cream at night, like my mother, and lots of fresh air.'

The girl remembered something. 'How's the new baby?'

'You mean Benjamin? He's fine. He's one year old already.'

'No, the second one. I read about it.'

Meg looked at her levelly. 'There isn't another one ... I lost it.'

The girl blushed. 'I'm so sorry ...'

'Don't be. Ben is an absolute joy for us both.'

Everard had grown impatient while these exchanges were continuing. 'Have you seen my new film, *Too Much Too Late*?' he asked the girl.

'I don't think so,' she replied '– but I saw you in that coffee advert.'

On glorious summer evenings they sipped beer in the gardens of country pubs. At one such place Everard asked for a pint and two straws. The barman handed over the straws without comment. The locals stared then, probably enchanted by the sight of two beautiful young people lovingly sipping from a single glass, rather than ogling two famous faces.

'Does it taste better like that?' one of the locals asked.

'It does – as long as she doesn't splutter and send stuff back into the glass!' Everard assured him.

'I don't think that's possible – but yuck anyway!' said Meg.

She was content.

Except that at the back of her mind was the thought that she should be doing more with Ben. She would go with Ben to the seaside. The outing was not a success. Greatly daring, Meg left Julia behind. She would look after Ben herself for the day.

The child resisted being pulled out of his nanny's arms; then as they set out for Scarborough he wouldn't stop crying. Meg could see from Everard's clenched jaw and fixed look as he drove the Healey that he was hating it, but he managed to say nothing.

Eventually Ben exhausted himself and fell asleep. Then Meg worried about the chill wind in the open car.

'Nonsense ... children are hardy creatures,' said Everard, who knew nothing about them. He refused to stop and put the top up. 'And no one catches pneumonia in the summer.'

The next problem was changing Ben's nappy. Where to do it and how to do it. They were on Scarborough seafront. Meg spotted the nearby ladies' toilet and decided to change Ben there.

'I'm sorry you can't come in and watch,' she told Everard. 'I'm not,' he replied.

Everything looked so simple when Julia did it. Meg failed utterly. Try as she would, the cloth was obviously not pinned together properly. Just as bad, now the original nappy was off she knew she couldn't reinstate it. The only way was to call the nanny. She carried a scarcely leak-proof Ben to the nearest phone box. With Everard refusing to help, Meg discovered the disadvantage of not having three hands. She needed two hands to change the nappy, and another hand to hold the phone.

Laying Ben on the none-too-clean floor of the booth, she got Julia to talk her through the stages. At each stage she told the nanny to hold on while she practised the manoeuvre on the hapless baby. Meanwhile, Everard stood outside looking around him with the air of a stranger who was simply waiting his turn to use the box.

Eventually the job was sort of done. The party, including a tired and grizzly Ben, returned to Lowmere. Meg found no satisfaction in the day. Looking after a child was a specialist job. It was best left to those who had the skills.

As the days slipped by, Everard was increasingly restive. He was restive for London and all the contacts he was missing there; he worried about what was happening in Hollywood while he was away.

'I'm not helping my career sitting up here,' he grumbled.

At last he had a call from his agent to say they wanted him in California as soon as possible. He looked and felt rejuvenated. The long, lazy summer days in the country, the rides across the estate, the walks in the gardens, the country pubs, Meg laughing, smiling, caressing, happy – all became just memories. Meg had trouble persuading him not to leave that instant. Instead, Everard would leave first thing in the morning.

Their love-making that night was especially inventive and tender, as if they were storing memories for the long separation. Repeatedly, Meg cried out in ecstasy as was her way. While most of her existed in a nowhere realm of bliss, a tiny part tried, without much success, to keep the sound down because of her parents in their room along the corridor. Everard, on the other hand, was uncharacteristically vocal. He was usually as silent as a mechanic servicing a straightforward car. Now he grunted and sighed, and he too lost all sense of time.

'Come with me to LA,' he said afterwards.

Meg, sated, said: 'Mmm ... lovely idea, my sugar-bun. Would we have a terrace overlooking the Pacific Ocean?'

'We would. High above the ocean.'

'And sunshine all the year round?'

'We would. Almost every day.'

'Freshly squeezed orange juice for breakfast every day?'

'Yes, that's automatic.'

'We'd go to all the best parties, and the most interesting people would come to ours?'

'Yes, yes. All of them.'

'And skiing in the Rockies in the winter?

'Whenever we want.'

Meg gave a long sigh. 'Oh Ev, London seems very dull after that. I'd give anything to do it. But you know I can't.'

'Why the hell not?' he asked, lurching into petulance.

She reminded him of her contract for two pictures to be made in Britain. And her concern that in Hollywood she would have nothing to do except kill time and wait for him to come home from the studio.

'Sweetheart, they'll eat you up over there,' said Everard. 'You'll have all the pictures you want. They'll go bananas over "Lady Meg Denby" *.'

'I'm not "Lady". You know that. Anyway, you can't just turn up and say "I've come to be in pictures". You have to be asked. Like you.'

Then there was the question of Ben. It wouldn't be

fair to uproot him, and she wouldn't want to be so far away from him.

Everard said: 'But you don't see much of him as it is. Two hundred miles or five thousand miles – what's the difference in the jet age?' He might have been talking about somebody else's son, not his own.

Meg burst into tears at this brutal reminder. And so the matter of her going to Hollywood drifted away.

They returned to London in the Healey the next day, the Jensen being garaged at Lowmere for the duration. The day after that Meg drove Everard to Heathrow.

'I'll miss you – madly and badly,' he told her theatrically. But by how much and for how long, Meg wondered.

At Wootton on the Isle of Wight, Bob Dylan – returning to performing after three years in semi-retirement – appeared before many thousands of festival goers. Meg wasn't one of them.

# FOUR

ARNOLD HAVERSTOCK was at his typewriter when Meg dropped into the flat in Wendover Street, Bloomsbury. It occupied the first floor of a Georgian house in one of the handsome terraces that abound in that part of London.

Haverstock's antique furniture was offset with brightly coloured abstract paintings on the walls. The polished floor was relieved with fine Turkish rugs. All was artfully arranged with just a suggestion of trying too hard for effect. Nothing had changed since Meg lived in this place three years ago.

Haverstock was 20 years older than Meg, an established author and a decorated war hero. She was with him for three years, until he started feeling more like her father than her lover. They drifted apart. Now their grand passion had evolved into a companionable friendship.

She had done much of her growing up in this house. Her early upbringing and education were typical of her time and class. She started life in the charge of a nanny, as her son Ben was now. Her parents were loving and relatively enlightened: Lady Chilcott saw her daughter not once a day as was customary but twice – a pattern Lord Chilcott followed when he was home from his political duties.

After preparatory school Meg was sent to Roedean as a boarder. Here came the first signs that her life would follow a different path from that mapped out for her. A stunningly pretty 15-year-old, she was spotted in the streets of Brighton by a scout for a photo agency. With her parents' reluctant consent, she became a successful model for teenage fashions. She wore her clothes so perfectly they might have been poured on – a gift she kept into adult life. Somehow she also contrived to do exceptionally well with her O levels, scoring nine good passes. Oxbridge began to look likely.

Lord Chilcott worried that his daughter was going off the rails. She still enjoyed a rough-and-tumble with her brother Thomas, two years older. She was turning into either a blue-stocking or a permanent tomboy, it appeared. A year at a Swiss finishing school was prescribed. To which Meg agreed reluctantly.

'It was the early Sixties and it was already obvious that finishing schools were on the way out,' she would say later. 'Presentations to the Queen finished in 1958, so what was the point of all that etiquette?'

She admitted: 'It was quite a fun year though.' Usually, she discreetly failed to mention that this in good part was because of a lad from the nearby village. Despite the best efforts of the dragons at the gate of the villa, they managed to become friends. Having lost her virginity to a boy in Brighton, she saw no reason to deny the Swiss lad. The couple were bereft when Meg went home – and soon forgot one another.

By now Oxbridge had lost its appeal. Meg, who as a child had loved dressing up and acting in plays of her own imagining, decided to become an actress. She was accepted for RADA, spending two years there. On the cusp of adulthood she was heart-stoppingly beautiful with a freshness that student life with its drink, drugs and sex left unmarked. It was no surprise when she fell into a starring part in her debut film. Two more starring film roles plus a leading part in a television series, The Image Benders, turned her into one of the best known names and faces in the country.

Meg had been at RADA only a few months when, aged 18, she met Arnold Haverstock. It was at a crowded end-of-term party. She kept noticing this remarkable-looking man who was working his way through every pretty girl in the room. Her turn would surely come.

He was remarkable in how different he was – for a start, at least ten years older than everyone else apart from a couple of tutors, who were their usual scruffy selves. This man wore a suit with a white shirt and a tie. He was solidly built but not especially tall. She guessed he seemed taller than he was because of the way he carried himself.

Haverstock saw this astonishing girl who was surrounded by an ever-changing cast of young men. She wore a flowing peasant dress with a headband containing her mop of hair. She often laughed, causing her long black hair to bounce around. Time was running out at the party. He must get to talk to her with or without her acolytes.

She happened to look across at the same time as his eyes found a way through the knot of young men. Their eyes locked, and they experienced simultaneous *coups de foudre*.

He went over to her and, as the previous speaker paused for breath, began: 'Amy invited me but she's not here.'

Meg didn't know any Amy at RADA. She wasn't sure that such a person existed. As a chat-up line it had the great merit of being unexpected.

'I'm sorry about that,' she replied. 'At least I'm here.'

With Haverstock's powerful presence the others naturally dropped away. They were left alone.

'How are you liking RADA?' he said, more conventionally now.

'It's certainly very different from amateur dramatics! The greatest thing is to perform with real material in front of genuine professionals,' she replied.

When he learnt that they were doing *As You Like It*, he said: 'And I know, you're playing Rosalind.'

It was a high-risk tactic but it worked. Yes she was.

'You'll be pushed to pass for a boy,' he observed.

Meg recognised this as a rather laboured compliment. 'I can do it when I try,' she responded lightly. 'I was quite a tomboy in my teens – my earlier teens, I mean. My father was unhappy about it.'

Haverstock couldn't be bothered with the obvious line that Daddy had nothing to be unhappy about now. 'In Shakespeare's time the women's parts were played by boys. So the joke would have been that Rosalind was played by a boy playing a girl playing a boy.'

'I never knew that,' said Meg.

'I can tell you more about how things were done in Shakespeare's day if you like.' He was pressing his advantage. 'It's noisy in here, but perhaps we can have a coffee after the party.'

He left her, having secured his prize. 'Who was that interesting man?' Meg asked her friend Julia after he had left her. 'Arnold something.'

'That was Arnold Haverstock, the famous author,' said Julia. 'He's a bit of all right for an oldie, isn't he?'

Within a fortnight and without her parents' knowledge, Meg had moved into the Wendover Street flat. An elaborate deception was in place to maintain the fiction that she still lived in a squalid house with Julia and two other girls.

'Don't worry, Meg,' said Julia. 'It frees up your room for other activities ...'

Haverstock proved to be an effective lover. He had none of the urgency of young men. Meg, who had never slept with anyone over twenty-five, was amazed that someone approaching forty had such vigour. In fact, it was surprising that he could manage it at all. He was nearly as old as her parents.

At the same time, he took her education in hand. They worked their way through the best of English literature, with excursions into other countries. 'You have all of the brains and none of the background,' he said with affection. 'If you'd stayed at the proper school instead of going to Switzerland, who knows where you'd be now?'

'Not with you, maestro,' Meg giggled. 'I'd be a formidable lady don at Oxford, praising Virgil and virginity to the girls in my charge.'

Haverstock had a special liking for the King James Bible, and set Meg to read great chunks of it.

'How did you enjoy that little exercise?' he asked her.

'I enjoyed it a lot,' she replied. 'It's like watching Shakespeare. The language is odd at first, but you quickly get the ear for it and then it seems entirely natural.'

'That book is three hundred and fifty years old,' he said. 'How many words didn't you know?'

'Hardly any. I was surprised.'

'No surprise at all. The King James more than any other book has made the English language we have today.'

# FIVE

THAT morning Haverstock presented himself in jeans, cowboy boots, crushed linen shirt and a flowing silk scarf. A Viva Zapata moustache completed the effect. A former diplomat, he used to be seen as reliably on the right politically. Then he went with the Zeitgeist and became an environmentalist. Largely due to Meg's influence, he dressed the part.

'What are you writing, cher maître?' Meg asked.

'I'm doing a piece for the Observer about the zero growth economy *,' he said. 'What's so good about unending growth year after year? I am what I consume, or I consume therefore I am ... What a prospect for humanity!

'Economics is a morally bankrupt science – he was talking to himself, or polishing a paragraph for the article – which wants us to buy stuff whether we need it or not. And what, pray, when the world runs out of resources to make it all?'

Meg, nodding, said: 'You ought to talk to Daddy about it! He's in politics.'

'From what I hear, I'd do better to aim at your MP brother Jeremy,' Haverstock replied, laughing. 'He's gung-ho for growth. For him helping the environment means having three courses for dinner instead of four. Uses fewer resources and less fuel in cooking. He's done his bit.'

'Don't be beastly! I'm very fond of Jeremy.'

'As it should be. But you can be fond of someone and still know their weak points,' said Haverstock.

'I suppose you're fond of me, but do I have any weak points?' Meg asked coquettishly.

'I never discovered any, but they must be there somewhere!' he responded. He rested his hand on her right thigh above the knee, where it was exposed by her miniskirt. He squeezed the thigh, then took his hand away. Meg recognised a playful gesture from which all sexual content had been drained.

Haverstock went on: 'And before you ask, *One Swallow at Midsummer* is doing very nicely, thank you. A film option has been taken already. Do you want to be in it?'

'Not if a casting couch is involved!' she said lightly.

'Miss Denby, how could you even think it!'

After they had coffee, she told him she would be speaking at the coming Vietnam rally in Hyde Park. 'Good for you, girl' was his response. He suggested some points to make:

'Ask who is our enemy in Vietnam – and answer your own question quickly before the audience start shouting answers. The Vietcong aren't our enemy. The North Vietnamese Army isn't our enemy. Even the Americans aren't our enemy. You'll get disagreement at that, and this is good. Pause while the people have their say; then tell them no, not even the Americans. The Chinese aren't our enemy. We're frightened of shadows with them. No, our enemy is – the US military-industrial complex. They are a small group of evil people who want the war and profit from the war. Beat them, and that's the end of the war. That should do it, I think.'

'That's powerful stuff!' said Meg. 'You ought to give

the speech yourself.'

'I'll be at the front of the crowd, waving.'

Marching groups of protesters converged on Hyde Park. They were noisy and, to judge from their banners and their shouts, angry. But Meg sensed none of the raw rage of the Grosvenor Square demonstration the year before. Perhaps the rage would come as the speakers whipped up the emotions of the crowd spilling out in the thousands from the Speakers' Corner area of the park.

Meg was angry about Vietnam and she felt no reason not to share her feelings. She wasn't frightened of speaking to large groups, but she had to admit that this was different. Its huge scale made her anxious. She hoped to see Haverstock among those close to the platform. There were plenty of Viva Zapata moustaches. His didn't seem to be among them.

Her fellow speakers were a trade unionist, a former British diplomat who had seen the light and a stridently left-wing MP. She was to speak first, as the youngest with the fewest credentials in the peace movement. Opening the show ... the worst spot! And it was on her all too soon. She felt she was going to throw up as she realised that the chairman was about to cue her in.

'Friends, comrades, we are here to make known how the people of this country feel about this wicked war,' he began, and paused confidently for the cheers that soon came, rippling through the vast crowd like the Severn Bore. 'It has backers in high places, which is why we must make our numbers count [cheers]. Few higher than the Right Honourable the Viscount Chilcott, former Tory Minister, panjandrum of the House of Lords, Lord Lieutenant of the North Riding of Yorkshire, owner of 4,000 acres. Never heard of him [shouts of 'No']? You can

## His Lordship's Disgraceful Daughter

bet your week's wages that the Government have as he presses them here and pushes them there as an arch supporter of America's colonial adventure [boos]. Well, I'm glad to say his daughter is cut from a different cloth. She knows the truth of it. She's with us – and she's with us now. Friends, comrades – the actress and campaigner Meg Denby [very muted response as the crowd waited to make up its mind].

Meg's thoughts were reeling. She hadn't expected this gratuitous attack on her father. It was a cheap shot the better to build her up. Why should Daddy have been mugged like that? He was no extremist. Many old people thought like him. Should she ignore the crude remarks? Should she defend him? How could she do that without destroying her speech; getting lynched even? She had dried in front of thousands. She realised that she couldn't find any words with which to begin.

Then she saw Haverstock. He had worked his way close to the platform. He gave her a nod of encouragement and mouthed the word 'enemy', which was to be the theme of her remarks. It jerked her into saying something:

'Friends, fellow campaigners, it's true my father and I have arguments over dinner ...' She hadn't meant this as a joke, but a huge gust of laughter rocked the crowd over which shouts of 'Dinner, by jove!' and the like could be heard. She had invited the very image of country house dining that she wanted to avoid. But it was all right. She sensed the crowd was with her.

Haverstock signalled a thumbs-up as encouragement. Now the actress in Meg took over, confident she could work the crowd.

She began again: 'I am young and the people fighting

this war are young. The people running this war are old. It's a war of the young set up by the old [supportive cheers] ... to fight an enemy that doesn't exist [cheers]. For who is our enemyit'snot [said quickly so no one could interrupt] the Viet Cong [shouts of 'No']. It's not the North Vietnamese Army [shouts of 'No']. It's not the Chinese [more muted agreement]. We're frightened of them, but they're even more frightened of us – or I should say the Americans [loud jeers]. But even the Americans aren't our enemy ...'

Here Meg made a theatrical pause, which elicited a range of responses with 'Yes they are' and the like predominating. Thanks to Haverstock's words and her dramatic flair, Meg knew she was carrying the crowd with her.

'No, the American people aren't our enemy,' she continued. 'Kids like us are protesting over there the same as here [cheers]. Even the airmen who carpet bomb defenceless Vietnamese villagers from their B52s, who pour Agent Orange on to their crops – they aren't the enemy either. They have their orders [shouts of derision].'

Meg made another pause. Into the silence a lone voice sounded loud and clear: 'Get to it, girl ... tell us who!' with a swell of laughter from the crowd.

'Yes, I will tell you,' she said. 'Our enemy is the small group of evil people behind this war – the US military-industrial complex [shouts of 'Yes'], aided and abetted by the British Government [huge, derisive cheers]. They want this war and they profit from this war. They sell their weapons and make their fortunes; they win their medals and bask in glory. BUT we can beat these evil people and we can end this war ... If we stand together and stay solid, friends and fellow campaigners, we can overcome!'

She stepped back from the microphone flushed and wide-eyed from the force of her own rhetoric. The crowd, similarly aroused, applauded wildly.

At the end of the rally, Meg made her way with Haverstock through the dispersing crowds. People shook her hand and slapped her back. No one wanted an autograph. This was Meg Denby the campaigner, not the actress. An elderly man said to her very simply: 'Vanessa and Jane couldn't have done it better.'

The newspapers and the three television stations all agreed that Meg was the star of the rally. Her remarks (with glamorous picture of the speaker in full flow) eclipsed the speeches of the trade unionist, the former British diplomat and a stridently left-wing MP.

Her father was not so impressed. Lord Chilcott asked to see her urgently at the House of Lords. As Meg entered his room she noticed that the day's newspapers were piled on the desk.

'Meg darling, I have to say that I'm worried about this,' he began, pointing to the papers.

'I didn't expect you to agree with me,' she replied.

'It's gone beyond our personal disagreements,' he continued. 'Haven't you thought how damaging this publicity is for your career? You don't want to get a reputation as a trouble-maker.'

Lord Chilcott had thought hard about how to play this scene with his spirited daughter. He knew that whatever approach he took was likely to be wrong. In this he was right.

'There are more important things than my career,' she snapped back.

'Darling, you can't mean that. You've always wanted to act. Don't you remember when you were a little girl you put on a play for us in which you did every part yourself!'

'Daddy,' Meg said, beginning to show exasperation, 'what is the point of this talk? I'm just expressing my opinions on *the* most important matter around ...'

'Ah, but you're doing more than that. You're campaigning, and you're trying to change government policy.'

'What if I am?'

'Look, you're a public figure now. Thousands hear your views through the press and broadcasting, and perhaps adopt them as their own. That makes the government's job harder. It's steering a difficult middle course between funking it on the sidelines of this important war and doing what the Americans want with consequent loss of British lives. It needs to carry public opinion with it. What you're doing is damaging and dangerous.'

'Damaging and dangerous?' she responded with amazement.

'Yes, damaging for the government's cause and dangerous for you.'

'How can it possibly be dangerous for me? No one's going to shoot me on the platform ...'

'I don't mean that.' Lord Chilcott stopped and seemed to seek inspiration by staring at the pile of newspapers on the desk.

'What is it, Daddy?'

'I had a phone call from the security people ...'

'You mean MI5 *, I suppose. Arnold said they were bound to take an interest. Let them!'

Now it was Lord Chilcott's turn to show exasperation. 'Meg, this is serious. This isn't a game. What you're trying to do is stir up opposition to a crucial part of Britain's foreign policy. The security people have it in their power to ruin you, professionally and personally. They aren't threatening you. They just suggested I ask you to lay off for everyone's sake including yours.'

It was advice that Meg was never going to take. Soon after that she left him. It was the first time he could remember when they had parted without her kissing him.

Walter Greening, the head of the studio where Meg's current picture, *As Far As the Eye Can See*, was nearly complete, was similarly unimpressed with her peace protests. 'These ideas of yours about Vietnam don't help this picture or you,' he told Meg.

She protested. 'I thought actors and actresses these days were supposed to show their social awareness by using their brains on important issues,' she urged.

'On *safe* important issues,' said Greening. 'Yes, that's great publicity. Talk about starving black babies or saving the environment or not wearing fur – but stay away from divisive issues like Vietnam. Every time you open your mouth on that subject, I lose audience. People will say "I shan't watch a picture with that dreadful girl in it".'

# SIX

It was raining at Kings Cross when a small group of protesters handed out anti-war leaflets. A dismal day in one of London's most dismal areas. Meg had tied back her long hair and hid it under a scarf. She also wore thick black spectacles, and in this way passed unnoticed. The others in the group were students except for Meg's friend Lucy Plessey and her six-year-old daughter Rosie.

Rosie's role was to make the group seem less threatening. She was to protesters what dogs are to beggars. She didn't hand out leaflets because using a child for politics was potentially alienating for the general public. In the same way, the organisers discouraged babes in arms because these suggested rampant free love.

Meg was pleased to find that few people refused to take a leaflet. Mostly they put them in their pockets without a glance; some threw the leaflets away, in a bin or on the ground, within sight of the group.

'If I was being paid to hand out this stuff I wouldn't mind what people did with it!' said Lucy.

'Don't be discouraged, Eeky,' said Meg, using her friend's pet name. 'Don't they say that if one in 10 persons changes her mind because of the leaflet, that's worth all the rain in London.'

'Mummy, you promised me an ice cream,' said Rosie.

Unnoticed by any of the group, a camera clicked twice in a nearby doorway.

The group was glad when their allotted two hours

were up and they handed on the baton of protest. They went to Meg's flat, which was near enough to walk to (although Rosie had to be bribed with a second ice cream halfway along the route).

The boys and girls disposed themselves comfortably in the living room. This mainly consisted of avoiding the chairs and using the floor. A couple immediately went off together.

'Why have those two gone into the bedroom, Mummy?' asked Rosie.

'I expect they've gone to discuss their plans for a big trip,' said Lucy.

'Talking of trips, have you got any stuff?' asked a young man called Nigel.

'Of course,' said Meg, bringing out the grass and handing round cigarette papers in which to roll it.

'Mummy, what's this funny smell?' Rosie asked.

'It's just some special sort of tobacco, darling,' said Lucy.

The next hour or so passed with nobody saying much. The couple emerging from the bedroom was taken as the cue to discuss practical matters.

'We need some headline-grabbing stunt,' said a girl called Kate. 'Like climbing Nelson's Column or hijacking a bus.'

'Man, all that stuff's been done already? Who cares about hijacked buses anymore?' a young man called Kieran objected.

'So what would you do?' Kate retorted.

Kieran hadn't prepared himself for a counter-attack. He was thinking about this when Lucy put in: 'Maybe there's other stuff we should be doing along with Vietnam. You know, women's lib, homosexuals' rights, the population explosion, poisoning the environment with chemicals ...'

'These are all manifestations of the prevailing capitalist paradigm,' said a young man named Hugo, who was doing a postgraduate degree in political science. 'Vietnam means they sell arms to fight the dirty Commies. Women are suppressed so they form a pool of cheap labour or in the case of housewives, no-cost labour. Queers * can't come out because there's no free speech because free speech threatens the System. An exploding population means more people to sell junk to, and no one cares about poisonous chemicals because we'll soon be dead.'

'Wow! But what can we do?' asked Kate.

Hugo replied: 'Change the paradigm! We can be the generation that pulls down the citadels of militarism and capitalism. Then really and truly all the other subsets of problems will fall into place.'

'Perhaps we should concentrate on leaflets for the time being,' said Meg.

'Hey Meg, can't you get some film stars to speak out?' Kieran suggested. 'That's the most valuable publicity. Look at all the publicity you got from your Hyde Park gig.'

'I can try,' said Meg.

She started by asking cast members and crew of *As Far As the Eye Can See* to sign a petition against the war. The approach was not a success. The director, Bert Brump, waved her aside without looking at the piece of paper.

'I don't sign petitions,' he said. Brump was an old-style journeyman director, as far removed from the socially engaged auteurs as the eye can see.

'Not even about Vietnam?' Meg persisted.

'Leave it to the politicians,' he said, walking away.

Some of the older actors and crew members were strongly right-wing, and declared that it was a good thing the Communists were being walloped.

'But they aren't ... all these lives are being lost for nothing,' said Meg. They still wouldn't sign.

Norman Fortescue, a leading character man in his fifties, was receptive enough to discuss the issue with Meg. He clearly had more than Vietnam on his mind as his gaze swung from her face to her breasts underneath the T-shirt to her thighs snug in jeans * and back again, like a searchlight tracking across the sky. He did nothing more than look, however, and at the end of Meg's explanation he told her sadly that he couldn't sign.

'I'm with you, darling, but it's more than my career's worth,' he said. '*They* wouldn't like it.'

'Who are *they*?' she asked.

'The security people, of course,' he replied. 'They are everywhere. They especially go for theatre folk because of our public prominence. I've known it before. Korea. Malaya. You're taking a great risk.'

'I doubt it,' said Meg.

Her co-star, Bob Curzon, readily agreed to sign. He was a Cambridge graduate who was able to lift his eyes above the next film script. 'Why not?' he said. 'People with any sort of public recognition should stand up and be counted.'

At the end of a hard day's canvassing she had obtained only five signatures. One was from a young actress, Alison Adams. She was 19, making her first picture and cast as the younger sister to Meg's heroine.

Meg had a heart-to-heart with the girl a few days

before when she heard her crying in the next dressing room. Shooting had finished for the day.

'Bert's not happy with my bedroom scene and says I must stay behind to reshoot it,' Alison explained between sobs. This was a scene where she had two long speeches, largely directed at the dressing table mirror. Meg was surprised by this news because she was in the scene too, although her character had little to do except listen to her sister.

'Everyone knows I made a hash of it – the crew, I mean. I feel I'm being kept in after school,' the girl sobbed.

'Reshooting a scene isn't the end of the world,' said Meg.

But Alison wasn't done. She saw her career disappearing when it had hardly started. 'Bert says he doesn't want to hold everyone else up, so he'll feed me the cues himself. I'll just freeze ... I'll make even more of a hash of it,' she wailed.

'I'll give you your cues,' said Meg.

The girl's anguish disappeared on the instant, replaced with a look of gratitude that was pathetic in its intensity.

'Would you really?' she said. 'Surely you have things to do.'

'Nothing that can't wait.'

'But you're the star. You shouldn't be reading people's cues,' Alison persisted.

'I don't mind at all,' said Meg. 'We're all in the same team.'

She wondered whether Alison was signing the petition to repay this small act of kindness. But no, she was evidently interested in the issues. By the end of their conversation she had agreed to join the leafleting group pounding the streets of Kings Cross.

# SEVEN

It was the last day of location filming for *As Far As the Eye Can See*. This was a drama about a girl who stumbles on a millionaire in disguise and wins his heart. Robert (Bob) Curzon, the co-star, was gloriously free of theatrical ego. He treated Meg like another Dame Peggy Ashcroft whose every utterance dripped acting wisdom. She put this down to the fact that, although about her age, he had entered the business later than she had. He had a way of gazing at her with rapt attention. Finding her a stunner clearly helped his appreciation of her dramatic and intellectual powers.

The company was shooting at a mansion in beautiful North Devon. Cast and crew stayed at a hotel in the small town of Great Torrington – except for the director, who was 'staying with friends' but who was suspected of treating himself to a superior hotel in nearby Bideford.

Bert Brump was delivering his usual craftsmanlike product. It made no claim to being great art. Even so Meg felt she needed to call his attention to a social gaffe in the script. Her character was seen entering a grand house with her chauffeur carrying the bags.

'It wouldn't be like that,' she told the director. 'The chauffeur wouldn't enter by the front door. The staff would take the bags, and the chauffeur would use a back door.'

'Says who?' said Bert. Then he remembered. 'Oh yes, you would know, wouldn't you?'

'Yes, I believe I would,' said Meg. She liked the idea

that he saw her simply as an actress, not a rich amateur playing at acting.

The hotel manager in Torrington, aware of the reputation of theatricals, had written into the contract that there was to be no smoking of any sort except for tobacco. She needn't have worried. As far as Meg knew, no joints had been smoked on or off the premises. Nor had she seen any evidence of bed-hopping. The shoot was a chaste affair all round.

Even the wrap party was half-hearted. People's thoughts were on the long drive back to London the next day. The area had until recently been laced with railway lines, but after the Beeching cuts taking a train from anywhere near Torrington was impossible.

Suddenly the party was over and Meg found herself alone in the room with Bob Curzon. The rest of the company were discreetly leaving the stars alone to get it on if they hadn't already. Actually, they had been friendly and enjoyed each other's company, but nothing more.

'That was a pretty dire meal,' said Bob.

'Mmm,' Meg acknowledged.

'I'm still hungry,' he announced. 'Come on, let's get a doner kebab. *'

'Or even one each!' Meg giggled.

He grabbed her arm and laughingly pulled her out of the room. Having spent a month in bed with her (while both wore swimming trunks under the blankets), the physical contact felt entirely natural.

Everyone in the small town seemed to know about the film being made in their midst. But beyond a few curious stares no-one bothered them.

'And chips with it, the greasier the better,' Bob told the Turkish man who was assembling their doners.

'That won't do my weight or my complexion any good,' Meg protested.

'Are you working tomorrow?'

'No but ...'

'Then eat, drink and be merry for tomorrow we – do nothing!'

They ate hungrily, squeezed on to a tiny table in the kebab shop.

'That was naughty but damned good!' said Meg. She lent her weight against his body. Responding, he put an arm across her shoulders. And left it there. She made no move to free herself.

'The night is still young,' said Bob. 'I'm not in the mood to go to bed. There's lots I want to talk to you about.'

'Like what? You've been talking to me all month.'

'Not seriously though. For example, I read about your speech at the Vietnam rally. Saw clips on TV too. You were magnificent.'

'Thank you for signing my petition.'

'Every thinking person – every young thinking person perhaps – should be against the war,' said Bob. 'It's the cause that defines our times.'

'Everard isn't interested in the war,' said Meg.

'Your fiancé? Perhaps he has to concentrate on building his career and doesn't have time for anything else,' Bob answered tactfully. 'He's a huge star after all.'

Then it struck him that Meg might take this as a reflection on her star status. 'As you are yourself,' he added. 'And you also find time for causes.'

He changed tack and asked her whether she had tried the local drink – Devon rough cider. Tastes were changing even in its county of origin. It proved hard to find a pub serving scrumpy. Eventually in the roughest or at least the humblest pub in Torrington they located it served direct from a wooden barrel behind the bar.

'Wow!' said Meg enjoying the sweet drink that promised a kick to follow. 'This is nothing like the cider that was the first alcoholic drink I was allowed at home. I was thirteen.'

'Whiteway's and Bulmer's? I'll say ... you're right about the kick. We must be careful. We don't want to have to get back to the hotel on all fours.'

'I didn't think careful was on your agenda. What are we doing in this unknown pub in the middle of nowhere and nobody knows where we are?'

'Is anybody threatening us, or even being nasty?'

'Everard would say they're being nasty,' Meg giggled. 'No one has asked for our autographs.'

But a couple of unnoticed flashbulbs went off from the direction of the bar.

Bob, feeling the cider, was emboldened to deliver the same sort of line that he said on screen. 'You know you're lethal, Miss Denby!'

She looked inquiringly at his curious choice of word.

'Yes,' he explained, 'you're a lethal combination of naturalness and sexiness. You look like a supercharged girl next door.'

She smiled, tacitly accepting the compliment, and said nothing. 'I need coffee,' she announced.

It was too late to obtain coffee at the hotel and almost everywhere else. They found themselves back at the tiny table in the kebab shop.

The talk drifted to books. As Meg suspected, Bob was a serious reader. He spoke about Paul Ehrlich's *The Population Bomb* *, and how he was deeply concerned about the virtually infinite growth of human numbers on a planet of finite resources.

'The ideal family is a childless couple with two adopted children,' he said, quoting a line he'd seen somewhere. 'We're not doing well between us. You have one and I have two – all natural.'

Walking back to the hotel, he took her hand. It lay there unresistingly.

'It's been a wonderful evening, Bob. After that dreadful wrap party,' Meg whispered as they stood in the bedroom corridor encased in its deep midnight silence.

'It doesn't have to end,' he replied, motioning with his eyes to the door of his room. She followed him in.

They didn't tear each other's clothes off. Bob pointed to the tiny en-suite bathroom – one of the few in the hotel – and said: 'Why don't you go first? Help yourself to towels if you need them.'

She admired his confidence with this gradual approach. He was in control of the event without the slightest suggestion of dominating it. So different from the puppy-dog manner he often showed around her. Then she reminded herself that, although young, he was a married man with two small girls.

Meg when she emerged had stripped down to her bra and panties, decorously covering herself with a bath towel. Bob in his turn came out of the en-suite fully naked. He paused briefly – was he vain enough to want Meg to admire him? – then moved towards her as if this was the most natural state.

He was noticeably shorter than Everard, but was still a perfectly adequate height for a leading man. About six foot exactly, she guessed. She rather liked being with someone who wasn't a hulk dwarfing her own respectable five foot eight.

Bob's physique was splendid. The stomach was flat, the buttocks were taut and the biceps, even at rest, rippled with latent power. His member was beginning to stiffen, but was far from erect.

What Meg coveted most after Everard's long absence was to be caressed by someone other than herself. This Bob gave her. He was a wonderfully gentle and thoughtful lover. His fingers played over every part of her body. She did the same for him. She could tell from his sighs that it was working for him, too.

His fingers reached down there but didn't linger, moving on to so far undiscovered areas. At one point as he turned, his erect member brushed her outer thigh. She responded with a groan. Her body had become one huge erogenous zone. His act of penetration was so gentle that she hardly knew it had happened. It was no abrupt change in the style and tempo of their love-making; merely one sensation among the many in this symphony of delights.

The next morning it was as if nothing had happened. The hotel car park was crowded with the company's cars being prepared for the drive home as well as a large lorry for the camera equipment and props.

Meg was loading the Austin Healey. Bob was doing the same with a family-friendly Ford Cortina.

He came over to her and they looked at each other straight in the eyes, not touching because of the others around them.

'Last night was wonderful in every way,' he said. 'I'll remember it forever – but it has to end here. You know that, darling, don't you? I'm completely committed to my family, and you have Everard …'

'Don't,' she cried. 'Don't say any more. On location doesn't count – that's what they say.'

A troubled frown crossed his face. 'But tell me it was wonderful for you, too.'

'It was more than wonderful,' she responded.

And then they hugged and kissed – the chaste embraces of friends, colleagues and siblings.

After he was gone, she found she was missing Everard more than ever. Meanwhile, a problem nagged at her like an abscessed tooth. She had stopped taking the Pill * when Ev left for America, and Bob had taken no precautions.

# EIGHT

THE line to California was of variable quality but this time it was excellent. 'You haven't come home secretly and are phoning from next door, have you?' Meg joked.

'If only I had, darling,' he said, but he called the answer into doubt by enthusing about his activities in Hollywood. The picture was going terrifically well; he went to a party or event every night; he was meeting everybody who mattered and no, he didn't know when he would be home.

'I miss you, Ev,' she said. She was desperately relieved that the pregnancy test had been negative. If the result had been otherwise, she didn't know how she could have talked to Everard without giving herself away. He would never have forgiven her.

'Sugarbun, I miss you *sooo* badly too,' he intoned. She heard laughter in the background. 'Just Jack and Anne dropping in for a sundowner,' he explained without having been asked. 'That's Jack Nicholson and Anne Bancroft, you know' – dropping the names of two of the biggest stars.

Everard was so transparent. He was childlike in the way he gloried in his fame and his social successes. Meg often asked herself why she loved him. Was Everard just a habit? She had fallen in with him when they worked together on *All in a Day's Work*. She admired his self-belief, his uncomplicated enthusiasms and his rise from a humble background, with Eton and RADA polishing the rough surfaces to a fine sheen.

'Anne' and 'Jack', however, reminded Meg of the ultimate reason why she loved Everard. Underneath, he was needy. Most of all, he needed her – and because he needed her, she needed him.

It was so different from Haverstock's intellectual angst and, for that matter, the absurd diffidence of the journalist Howard Jenkins, with whom she had somehow found herself involved. More than that in fact, she acknowledged. She had been ready to marry him. It was he who bolted. Meg, who was given to self-analysis, asked herself again why she had done that. She had been hurt when Haverstock threw her over, and after Everard's erraticness Howard was simply *there*. She was carrying Ben. The expression 'honour of the family' was directed at the unmarried mother-to-be. Had she really fallen for that? In 1968? At least she had been spared the disaster that marriage to Howard would have been.

She felt neither anger nor grief about the end of her relationship with Howard. She felt nothing. Later, though, when she was touring the country with plays for the Grosvenor Company, she had enough curiosity to want to see him again.

She sent him a letter at the Messenger office, knowing he would instantly recognise her large sloping hand.

*Dear Howard*

*We are touring in Yorkshire [Meg wrote]. Try to get to the Saturday matinee – she gave the date – We can meet in my dressing room after the show if you like.*

*Love*

*Meg*

She enclosed a ticket.

She wondered if he would come. She imagined him

agonising over the decision, but she knew he would. Meg was enchanting as ever that afternoon, and was radiant as she took a large helping of applause at the curtain call.

He found her at her make-up table when he entered the dressing room.

'Howard, you came! I'm so glad.' He found himself unable to utter a word.

He looked older and rather tired, as if he was still recovering from the tumultuous events of the past months. Meg looked exactly as usual. If she had suffered a trauma from the aborted wedding, unrecognised even by herself, it didn't show. The long black hair fell on to the shoulders as always. She had changed out of a billowing period costume into jeans and a T-shirt a size too small. The jeans as always moulded themselves to her thighs.

She hugged him closely, and wasn't sorry to feel his hardening against her jeans.

'Meg, I can hardly bring myself to face you,' he managed at last.

'But you have.'

'I wanted so many times to contact you – to explain. But I never could. I still haven't forgiven myself. I'm so ashamed.'

'You don't need to be,' she answered lightly. 'You did what you felt you had to do. We've both lived to tell the tale.'

She was aware of giving him absolution. He seemed to need it.

'And the baby?' he asked.

'Ben. Benjamin. He's well. He's a handful, but a real delight.'

Seeing Howard's continuing discomfiture, Meg said:

'Why don't we have some tea – the universal panacea? And why don't we sit down? Or at least you sit down while I make the tea?' A sink and taps stood in a corner, with an electric kettle.

This broke his spell of embarrassment. 'How did you know where to find me?' he asked.

'Daddy saw an article of yours in the Messenger. We guessed you were back with them,' said Meg as she bustled with the tea things.

'How are your parents?'

'They're fine. Everything the same. Lowmere the same. Jeremy is still an MP, Thomas is still the playboy of the Western world. Sheila's history, but he has another actress in tow. Oh, and Daddy's finished his memoirs at last. He's to speak at a Messenger literary luncheon. Are you still eagerly reporting them?' She gave a pointed half-smile.

'Not anymore. They made me deputy news editor.'

'That sounds cool. Congratulations. And how are Jack and Pauline?'

'My parents are both well, thank you. They speak of you. They think you're a very nice person.'

'How little they know me! But they're very nice people, too!'

She really ought to tell Howard about the baby. Jack and Pauline would be rejoicing at being grandparents.

Howard had fallen silent. He was becoming choked by thoughts of what might have been. Images of Lowmere and the Bloomsbury flat rose up to assail him. He thought of how he had acted decisively to bring about that first date at the Fishermen's Rest, and of the aftermath of the premiere when Meg had brought him into her life. Christ, what am I doing here, he asked himself.

Meg picked up her teacup, and made a little play of sipping from it. 'I'm very happy,' she announced. 'Are you happy, Howard?' She allowed herself the pleasure in leaning back in the chair and casually spreading her legs in those poured-on jeans, knowing it would arouse him.

'I think so,' he replied. 'I'm happy to be in this job. I've come to accept my limitations. I'm not in your league, Meg. We can't all be in the first eleven.'

'What bollocks!' said Meg, who as Howard remembered had an earthy turn of phrase when she needed it.

'Look, you're an artist and I'm a plodder. I no longer torture myself with thoughts of creative writing. I shall never write a novel, you know. Our marriage would never have worked.'

'Have you found someone?' she asked. He noticed she didn't say 'someone else'.

'I believe I have.'

'Cynthia Hallett?' she hazarded. He had told her about his last girlfriend back home in Bristol.

'Yes, Cynthia Hallett. I met her by accident in Bristol a couple of months ago.' He wanted her to know that Cynthia had nothing to do with their break-up. Oh Meg, Meg! He was tortured with thoughts of what he had thrown away.

'And how about you?' he managed to ask.

'I'm with Everard. We're very happy. And after a pause: 'We're expecting our second child.'

Howard was visibly puzzled. 'But, Meg,' he began ... ' Then the penny dropped. 'And I thought Benjamin was mine.'

'I never said so,' she answered gently.

Everard was droning on about his social successes in

California. It was more than Meg wanted or needed to know.

'What's happening with the protest movement over there?' she asked.

'The protest movement?' he echoed as if he'd been asked what types of breakfast cereal were to be found in the local supermarket. 'Lots of demos and sit-ins all over town, I think. I've been too busy to follow it closely.'

With the shooting for *As Far As the Eye Can See* completed, Meg found herself at a loose end. There was no sign from the studio of the next contracted picture. She missed Everard terribly, and the things they did together – the premieres, the parties, the exhibitions, the trips to the country (take your pick, the Healey or the Jensen), just being companionably together in the flat – although Everard dashed off by himself so often that they didn't do much of that.

She never knew where he went or when he would be back. 'I need fresh air,' he would say. 'We're not doing anything tonight, sweetheart, are we? I'll be back when I'm ready.' It was a provoking habit, although she couldn't help remembering that she had done much the same to Howard Jenkins.

Meg was not over-fond of her own company. She couldn't do most of these social activities by herself. Her friend Eeky was busy with her shop and her daughter while Tommy Radicek, always a willing walker, was shooting a picture in Austria. Arnold Haverstock had a new love interest. Even if the woman allowed it, she (Meg) wouldn't demean herself by asking for him as an escort. The leafleting crowd weren't presentable or sophisticated enough. She thought of Alison Adams, but on the whole better not. Alison, with the intensity she had already demonstrated with the reshooting episode, would expect too much of her. Meg wasn't ready for a new best friend.

London was in any case too hot. Relief was to be found in stripping down to almost nothing in the parks, but summer tourists clogged the streets and turned the Underground into an oven. Fumes from buses and cars hung heavily in the muggy air. So Meg retreated to the place where she was always relaxed – Lowmere.

The days fell into a comfortable pattern. She rose late. She saw Ben twice every day. He seemed to treat her the same as any other amiable visitor bearing sweets and small gifts. She took him on an outing to Scarborough but, mindful of the previous time, brought the nanny, Julia, with them. In the mornings she rode or walked by herself; in the afternoons she read books. Lord and Lady Chilcott were often out in the evenings. Meg thought of Julia and Ben upstairs in the nursery suite, but in the end took her dinners alone in a small sitting room.

She became worried by Everard's silence. She rang his apartment but he was always out. Eventually he came through, with the usual raucous sounds in the background. He wasn't in a chatty mood.

'Another party, Ev? Life's a non-stop party over there. Anne and Jack again?' she teased.

'Not this time,' he replied without saying who he was with.

'Where are you?'

'Just some bar with a guy from the film.' He clearly wanted to change the subject. 'What are you doing at Lowmere?'

'We finished Eyeful [this was their nickname for *As*

*Far As the Eye Can See*]. I'm resting, as they say. I feel great.'

But in truth she was bored.

'Kiss Ben for me,' Everard remembered to say as he rang off. The short call left Meg feeling more unsettled than she was before he phoned.

One evening Lord Chilcott came into the drawing room, where Meg and her mother were awaiting the call to dinner, looking bewildered.

'A group of about twenty women are pitching tents by the West Gate,' he announced.

'Are they gipsies?' asked Lady Chilcott.

'I don't think so. Johnson [he was the land agent] has spoken to them and they said Miss Denby told them to come.'

'Oh them,' said Meg.

'What do you mean, "Oh them"?' her father demanded. 'Who are they and why are they here? Do you know them?'

'I don't know them as such. I met them in a pub,' Meg replied. 'They've been attending a conference in York, and had nowhere to stay, I told them I was sure it would all right for them to stay here.'

Lord Chilcott's customary phlegm deserted him. 'Really, Meg, you might have mentioned it to Johnson or me. Secondly, what about washing facilities – or is that considered old-fashioned ...?'

'Oh Daddy!'

'And thirdly, you know I'm unhappy about you taking part in Vietnam protests, but to bring those people here is asking too much!

'"Those people", as you call them, are nothing to do with Vietnam,' said Meg. 'They're from the women's movement. Their conference was Emancipating Women in the Workplace.'

For Lord Chilcott, this was hardly any better.

Meg reflected that dinner conversations often took a difficult turn at Lowmere. She wished her brother Thomas was there. As an investment banker and London man about town, he was no mould breaker; but he was unstuffy and would have supported her. On this occasion it was Lady Chilcott who raised a delicate subject.

'What are your and Everard's plans?' she asked. Meg knew what her mother was getting at but played stupid. 'When are you getting married?' Lady Chilcott was forced to add.

'I don't think we are. We're happy as things are. Neither of us believes in a ring on the finger and a ring through the nose!'

Lord Chilcott, who struggled with the Sixties Zeitgeist, spluttered into his coffee. 'You didn't feel that way about Howard Jenkins. You were ready enough to marry him.'

'And I regret that,' said Meg. 'I was swayed by your "honour of the family" argument. And look where it got me!'

Her father said: 'Family honour's important. I make no apology for that, Nor is it good for Ben to be brought up as illegitimate ...'

'Daddy, this is 1969, not 1869!'

Lady Chilcott interjected: 'Even so, darling, have you thought about marrying Roger?'

Sir Roger Hudson was a wealthy farmer whose land adjoined Lowmere's. He and Meg were the same age, having known each other from early childhood. She had always viewed him as another brother, or perhaps a first cousin.

'Why would I want to marry Roger? Don't you understand I love Everard?'

'Perhaps Everard doesn't love you enough to marry you,' Lord Chilcott observed. 'Roger would give Ben a name. It would be suitable in every way.'

'Suitable but not right,' said Meg.

Two days after this conversation she ran into Roger while shopping in Ripon. They hadn't seen each other for a year. She was happy for the distraction of having lunch with him.

Roger led the way, as she knew he would, to the Old Rectory, a quirky restaurant where they had enjoyed meals together in the interlude between Arnold Haverstock and Everard Hughes. The owner and principal chef, Monsieur Charles, was known for his good days and his bad days in the kitchen. Such was the superb quality on his good days that the regulars were ready to risk the bad days.

'How's filming?' asked Roger when they reached their table – an unsubtle opening that was typical of him.

'How's farming?' Meg smiled.

'Don't answer a question with a question! I want to know all about your mad, wicked life in London.'

'Not so wicked with Everard away. He spends most of the time in Hollywood at the moment. I've finished my latest. The premiere will be quite soon actually.'

'You'll be sensational,' Roger said. They were seated side by side. He laid his hand gently on hers, but she pulled it away quickly.

'It's time we ordered,' he said levelly.

Monsieur Charles was having one of his good days,

but food couldn't overcome Meg's feeling that coming to lunch had been a mistake. Roger talked at length about crop prices and the shortcomings of the Milk Marketing Board. 'It's a responsibility taking over Lewis's land,' he intoned. (Lewis was the uncle from whom he had inherited the estate.) The former delight of the hunt balls, the man who was famously Unsafe in Taxis *, had become boring.

Enough of the old instincts remained that several times their legs touched under the table. Not content with ankles brushing, he somehow managed to get his thigh alongside hers. She felt the roughness of his tweed trousers on her tights. If only it were Ev – but Ev wasn't given to touching women under tables, or at least not her. Roger's touch was as unwelcome as a brother's. She twisted her leg away from his, saying nothing. Affecting not to notice, he carried on talking without a pause.

Over coffee he returned to the subject of Everard. He said: 'I'm glad you and Everard and Benjamin are happily settled as a family.' She didn't believe him, and he was obviously fishing for some sort of denial.

'Yes we are. Ben is a great joy. Despite Ev's commitments in Hollywood he spends as much time as he can with Ben at Lowmere.' This was totally untrue.

'And what about you, Roger?' Meg continued. 'Do you have someone special?'

'Yes I do,' he said. He looked her hard in the face and placed a hand in hers. This time she didn't pull away.

'It can't be,' she said gently. 'You know that.'

'More's the pity,' Roger responded.

# NINE

EVERARD was in high spirits when he returned from Hollywood. The picture was going to be a huge success; his agent was already discussing two more; Anne, Jack and the rest of the crowd were so welcoming he couldn't wait to get back there. Even the baking London late summer weather couldn't compare with California's. 'Too muggy,' he said.

'All that's lacking is you,' he told her one afternoon as they lay in a rowing boat on the Thames at Richmond. He had surprised her with his skill at the oars, but for the moment the boat had to look after itself.

'Ev, you know I can't,' she replied. 'Not yet. Perhaps soon.'

And there the matter drifted like the boat.

While he awaited the call back to California, Everard was content to spend lazy days with Meg at the flat, save for his habit of disappearing for 'fresh air'. They spent hours doing nothing, listening to music on Radio One, smoking dope, eating whatever the cupboard and the fridge fortuitously provided (often baked beans), drinking wine whenever they felt like it even for breakfast – making love.

Everard's appetite in that department never waned. His recovery powers were astonishing. Meg lost count of how many times she came each day. He was a most considerate lover. At times his touch was like a woman's, she thought. He never forced himself upon her until she was ready. At these times she knew the real Ev – the virtuoso eager to please. At other times, however, he seemed to take pleasure in holding back until she was begging for it; it was as if he wanted her to gag for it.

Nature had a marvellous way of equalising the benefits of sex, Meg told herself. Women might pay for their moment of pleasure with nine months of pain and handicap, yet had an almost limitless capacity for thrills. Men took their pleasure and could forget about it, except they were spent sometimes for hours, sometimes for days. Pathetic. And sad for them. This was where Everard was unique in her experience.

And now with the Pill women could have it all – pleasure with no risk of pain to follow. Yes, she was happy she was a girl.

Meg was horrified when Everard suggested anal intercourse. He couldn't bring himself to say it straight out. 'An opening we haven't tried before' was how he put it.

'What do you mean?' she questioned. 'We've done them all.'

'All bar one.'

Then the penny dropped. 'Absolutely no ... it's a horrid, disgusting suggestion,' she exclaimed. 'I'm ashamed to hear you say it.'

'It's not horrid and it's not disgusting,' he said petulantly. 'It's all the thing in Hollywood, I can tell you.'

'Then it can stay there!'

'Don't you want to try new things? It doesn't hurt. It's a very understanding orifice!'

She didn't care to think too deeply about how he knew these things. He had told her he lost his virginity at 13. There had been many lovers before Meg, but he was never willing to supply details and barely even names.

After she again refused the suggestion, his manner changed into a sneer. 'This is the Sixties when anything goes and everything's all right. But not for you ... you're back in the *Eighteen* Sixties!'

He left the flat immediately at that, and was away for hours.

Their relations, damaged by the incident, had recovered in time for Vivien and Amy's party. They were lesbians who were building reputations as character actresses on TV. Vivien, whose family had money, was the fortunate tenant of a riverside flat at Putney. The balcony doors were open to the beautiful evening, with the strains of Procul Harum's Whiter Shade of Pale * drifting across the darkening river.

Meg and Everard squeezed through the crush to find the drinks table. Everard drifted away and Meg, momentarily alone, decided to enjoy the cool of the evening. She had stepped out on to the balcony before she realised that one of the occupants was Bob Curzon. The other was a plainish young woman who didn't seem like an actress, character or otherwise.

'My wife Meryl,' said Bob, introducing the two women. He seemed to be quite unconcerned by the situation. On location doesn't count.

'Are you in the business too?' Meg asked Meryl.

'I'm an academic. At Imperial. Bob and I met at Cambridge.'

'You teach English but you should be teaching women's studies,' Bob joked. 'Betty Friedan * is far more relevant than Jane Austen.'

'Rubbish!' said Meryl. 'My husband has odd ideas. Jane Austen was a proto-feminist. Don't be fooled by the surface stuff about women defining themselves by marrying Mr Right. Follow the money, Jane says. A man chases a girl until she catches him *, as the song has it.'

Meg, who had never seen Jane Austen as a feminist, was fascinated, but before she could pursue the matter Meryl had drifted off saying she must 'grab a word' with someone.

'Do you want to dance?' Bob asked as the haunting Procul Harum tune continued. 'Bach is hard to resist done this way.' He'd hardly spoken when the anthem of the Summer of Love gave way to the bouncy Waterloo Sunset *.

'Too lively for me. I'd sooner talk,' Meg said. Her sexual feeling for this man had deserted her, handsome as he was. Perhaps it was his trusting wife and the mention of the sisterhood. But he was an interesting and well informed talker. She missed that part of her life with Haverstock. It was a gap that Everard couldn't fill.

Bob said: 'We can talk about our film or we can talk about Jane Austen. Or Betty Friedan ...'

'A women's group who camped at Lowmere recently talked a lot about Betty Friedan. They think *The Feminine Mystique* is terribly important.'

'It *is* terribly important,' Bob agreed. 'Her ideas about the stifling effect of marriage and housewifery on educated women really spoke to me. She calls it "the problem that has no name".'

'They give up their own careers, and then a few years later the husband runs off with someone else,' said Meg, who was familiar with the book.

'I'd never ask that of Meryl. Or run off with someone else for that matter,' Bob added with a laugh.

'Anyone I marry will have to accept my career,' said Meg.

'Quite right. And while we're on the subject you should keep an eye on Gloria Steinem.'

'Who's she?' Meg asked.

'She's very much the coming woman of American feminism. We'll hear lots about her. She's radical and she's stunningly beautiful – very like you, in fact.'

Meg saw yearning in his uxorious eyes. The compliment fell like a stone into the discussion of feminism, but she decided to let it go. 'Thank you, kind sir!'

'Gloria has published an article that's making big waves,' Bob continued. 'She calls women's liberation the next big cause after black power. It's going to be huge here too. Vietnam will end one day, but the subjection of women will still be with us.'

This wasn't Meg's view of things. 'Don't you think the barriers are coming down so fast that in a very few years the housewife model will be dead and gone; men and women will be equal at work and in the home?'

'I'd like to think so but I doubt it,' said Bob. 'So why don't you be the British Gloria Steinem?'

'Vietnam takes up all my time when I'm not working.'

'They're not really separate causes. Women and Third World peasants are groups united in oppression. Blacks, too.'

'That's what Hugo always says,' Meg reflected, thinking about the theoretician in the Vietnam group.

'Take abortion,' Bob pursued. 'Despite being legal now, society still makes women feel guilty about not pursuing a pregnancy even though this will define her life in ways she doesn't want to go. Gloria had an abortion and has spoken openly about it. She says she doesn't feel guilty. She wasn't going to let things happen to her; she was going to take responsibility for her own life.'

'I wish I'd had her guts,' said Meg.

'Surely you don't regret Benjamin?'

'Benjamin, no. But I got pregnant again. I regretted that. It was too soon. Then I lost it. If I hadn't she – they told me it was a girl – would have turned my life upside down.'

'I never knew,' said Bob.

Meryl reappeared. 'You two still at it? What film gossip are you swapping, I wonder. Come on, Bob. I want to dance.' They were gone.

Meg would be with Bob at the premiere of *As Far As the Eye Can See*, probably work with him again, but there would be no more book talk, one to one, and certainly not another encounter like the one at Great Torrington.

She spotted Alison Adams dancing with a rake-thin boy even taller than Everard. With his beanpole figure the boy looked like an overgrown 16, but no doubt was older. Alison was fresh-faced and laughing. She reminded Meg of herself a few years before. At 24 she felt the years beginning to press. Had she wasted her most joyous years on a relationship with a man 20 years older than her – a relationship that was bound to fail?

She felt a tap on her shoulder. It was Vivien. 'Would you care to dance?' she said.

'Why not?' Meg replied.

She didn't recognise the tune.

'It's new – just got it today,' said Vivien. 'He Ain't Heavy, He's My Brother *.'

The slow number was an invitation to smooching. Meg wished she was dancing it with Bob Curzon.

She asked Haverstock about Jane Austen as a feminist.

He wasn't persuaded. 'We don't have to read everything for a sub-text,' he said. 'Austen heroines are looking for Mr Right and having got him they live happily ever after. Even the spirited Emma in the eponymous novel ultimately finds her salvation in marriage. The books reflect the reality of their times that marriage was the only "career" for women.'

'Except writing books,' Meg quipped.

'Quite so, little star. And Austen was by no means the first. Even in her day a few talented women were able to carve out independent paths.'

This brought Haverstock to one of his favourite themes. 'Now if you want a proto-feminist of the period try Anne Bronte and *The Tenant of Wildfell Hall*,' he said. 'Anne – the least considered of the Brontes.'

Meg gave him a suitably quizzical look.

He explained that the tenant of the title was a woman, living at Wildfell Hall alone except for her young son.

'That would have been a shocking idea in its day,' he said. 'Even more shocking was the fact that she had left her husband because he mistreated her – and the author's evident approval of her action. Yes, you want to make sure your women's group have read *The Tenant of Wildfell Hall*.'

'I don't have a women's group,' Meg objected.

'Sounds to me as if you soon will. It doesn't have to be *either* Vietnam *or* women's liberation. The NVA and the Viet Cong will win, of course. Perhaps it will take ten years. But however long it takes, women's issues will still be with us.'

At that point Meg decided to become a women's libber.

# TEN

EVERARD burst into the flat in great excitement. 'Ken's got us an advertisement for national television ... worldwide, in fact!' he said.

Meg knew the agent was resourceful in opening up all possibilities, but she couldn't get worked up about a TV commercial.

'What's so wonderful about that?'

'Full production values,' he carolled. 'Not any old TV advert. Bert Brump will direct. Our face recognition will be enormous all over the world. They plan a series ... we'll be known as the Tundra gin couple.'

'I hate gin,' said Meg.

'Don't be silly. You don't have to drink it. Anyway, it's water they use for the advert. And it's *the* drink of the moment.'

'You don't have to persuade me,' said Meg. 'If it's that important to you, I'll do it.'

'And the money's great,' Everard enthused.

Meg had to admit that the advertising agency was throwing a lot of (the client's) money at this advertisement. For the shoot she found herself surrounded by the crew and equipment to be expected for a feature film.

Bert Brump, the director, showed no enthusiasm to be working with his two famous names. He showed no enthusiasm for anything about the project but, journeyman that he was, he intended to do a good job.

'This has to be stylish,' he announced. 'Gin's a stylish

drink. So they tell me. What would I know? We have this golden lad and lass (gesturing at Everard and Meg), and they're deeply in love, and they're expressing it by drinking Tundra gin. Hmmm.'

His expression and tone of voice suggested how absurd this idea was.

'We need an exotic location,' he went on. 'What can they provide here? Barbados, Tahiti, Borneo, Iceland ...'

'Excuse me, Bert,' said a girl called Debbie, who was from the agency. 'They're on a beach actually. The client wants somewhere warm. He wants them to be in beachwear. Adds to the sexiness.'

'Scrub Iceland,' Bert decreed. He picked up the storyboard. 'What's this? They're on a beach sipping gin through two straws in a single glass. Even I know that's not stylish! You do that when you're teenagers drinking a milk shake. These are supposed to be stylish people savouring a sophisticated drink!'

Bert was earning his money today. 'Thank you very much,' said Debbie. 'Of course you're right. I'll get back to the client and bring you a new storyboard ...'

'To hell with that,' the director replied. 'Let's just get on with it. But doing what?' He looked inquiringly at everyone in the studio.

Meg had a brainwave. 'Why don't we cross arms? Everard and I hold a glass for the other person, with his left arm crossing my right arm, or the other way round ...'

Bert looked at Debbie, who nodded. 'Been done before,' he said. 'But what hasn't?'

And so the shoot carried on. Later the images would be joined by this year's slogan. Last year it was TUNDRA GIN: IT'S GREAT WITH ICE. This year it was to

be TUNDRA GIN: A STEPPE CHANGE IN PLEAS-
URE.

Meg could hear Haverstock groan when she told him.

Soon after the advertisement shoot Everard left for Hollywood. Thus he would be away for Meg's premiere. He said: 'I'm so sorry, sweetheart. I wouldn't have missed it for the world.' She knew the very opposite was true. The world was exactly what he'd missed it for. His career versus her moment of glory.

Meg had to decide who would accompany her at the event. For her last picture – Everard once again being away – she had been on the arms of Tommy Radicek, the film director, and Howard Jenkins, the journalist. Now Tommy was out of London and Howard – well, she had no hard feelings about him, but he was a mistake she didn't care to resurrect.

After reviewing and dismissing the idea of Arnold Haverstock (sad even to ask) and her agent Ken (even sadder), she settled on the choice of her friend and former flatmate Lucy Plessey.

'People might think you were making a statement ... they might put a – well, certain construction on it,' said Lucy?

'And if they do? Aren't we supposed to be beyond petit bourgeois ideas these days? This is feminism in action. I don't care what people think. Do you?'

'No,' said Lucy. 'I'm planning my dress already.'

Meg's picture, *As Far As the Eye Can See*, was a bid to capture the continuing spirit of Swinging London *. When she wasn't at parties or waltzing through the streets in the latest fashions (her budget stretched a long way for a ordinary girl), Meg's character worked in an estate agent's. She went to immense trouble to sell a tiny one-bedroom flat – the cheapest property on the agency's books – to a man (played by Robert Curzon) who plainly could afford nothing better. The man turned out to be a widower millionaire who was buying a pied-a-terre for his niece. He was so impressed by Meg's commitment to such a modest deal that he allowed her to sell him a magnificent country mansion, with land as far as the eye can see. And installed her in it as his wife.

'An old-fashioned weepie, and all the better for it,' the film's director, Bert Brump, had declared.

Lucy had gone to huge trouble for the premiere. With her long face, shortish stature and solid build, she was never going to rival Meg. She was, however, unrecognisable from the figure who slopped around her bookshop in baggy pullover and jeans.

Meg was dazzling. Her cascading black hair had been restyled to sit closer to the face. Her ballgown in virginal white was accessorised in teal. Lucy complemented her friend in dove grey.

On her fourth premiere, Meg was used to the flashbulbs and the crowds. Lucy, at her first premiere, appeared serenely untroubled. If the guests or the crowd thought it odd for two women to make an entrance arm in arm, no one said so. Nor did the press reports the next day, actual or implied.

Alison Adams with the lanky boy from the party slipped in almost unnoticed. Another huge cheer went up for Bob Curzon, with his dowdy wife on his arm.

The film was heading for success at the box office. Laughs came in the right places. Meg sensed that the audience was absorbed in the story. Afterwards, the congratulations. 'Darling, you were wonderful! 'Simply stunning! 'You get better and better!' No way of knowing whether the praise was genuine or not.

She hadn't exchanged a word with Bob Curzon or the director all evening. She had little chance to do so now. They each had their own circle of well-wishers. Even Lucy, nothing to do with films, had a group with her. She was making them laugh although Meg wondered what was so funny about secondhand book-selling.

She noticed a head well above everyone else's. It belonged to Alison Adams' escort, with Alison herself alongside. She introduced the head and its owner as Tony. 'We were at school together,' she explained.

'Stage school?' Meg asked, curious about who Tony was.

'Gosh no, I haven't been to one of those,' said Alison. 'It was our grammar school at Sevenoaks.'

The picture was clear. Respectable middle class, Home Counties background. The wellspring of Alison's sweetness. A school romance, perhaps the first for them both. They would have graduated to sex eventually but were always careful with contraceptives. Tony would now be on the way to being an accountant or a lawyer. He would be fascinated by cars and play sport heartily at weekends. Alison had already moved beyond Tony's orbit. Both parties determinedly kept the relationship going, but it couldn't last.

'I didn't go to stage school either,' said Meg.

The others in the group around her had moved away, feeling instinctively that the performers should be given space.

'Wow, so you didn't go either!' Alison breathed into the remark wonderment that anyone could be that good without stage training.

'You were fantastic, Meg,' she went on. 'I wish I could

do half of what you can do. I so admire you.' The girl was very naive and had an advanced case of hero worship.

Tony had been gawping at Meg while this exchange was going on. He was frozen in the presence of beauty and fame.

'What did you think of the picture, Tony?' Meg asked.

He coloured. 'Well, I thought it was – er – well [reaching for a word worthy of the occasion] engrossing.'

'Engrossing? That's what lawyers do,' said Meg laughingly.

Tony looked blank.

'Don't worry about it. I'm just teasing you. I'm glad you enjoyed the show.'

A short, bald man pushed through the outer ring to Meg's side. 'That was magnificent, Miss Denby!' he exclaimed in an American accent. 'You not only caught the spirit of Swinging London; you *are* Swinging London. Look at me (that's you, I mean) ... I'm young, I'm happy and this is London, the most excitingest city on earth right now!'

He handed her his business card, announcing him as Harold Cohen from the Harold Cohen Agency. 'I represent Monumental Pictures here in London. We can't speak now, but I'd like to call you.'

The man could be anybody. Who were Monumental Pictures? Meg knew that the first rule of theatre was not to give out your private address or phone number. She gave him her agent's office number.

Another, scruffy man came forward. He was Joe Johnson, freelance journalist. 'Meg, I'd like to set up an article about you,' he said. 'How do I contact you?'

She knew better than to ask freelances who an article was for. They simply invented the most impressive or the most likely publication. The only test was whether an editor had commissioned the article. Meg couldn't be bothered to pursue the matter. She gave Joe Johnson the agent's phone number.

She went home and thought no more about either approach. In this she was wrong.

Ken the agent phoned next morning. He said: 'You'll be hearing from Harold Cohen, the man you spoke to last night.'

'You gave him my personal phone number?'

'You'll be glad I did. He's a talent scout for Monumental Pictures.' Sensing Meg's question, he added: 'They're a big player in Hollywood. They want you to go out to California for a screen test. Tomorrow – or sooner.'

Her second call of the morning was from the London bureau of Time magazine.

'We've heard from Joe Johnson, one of our best correspondents,' the editor began. 'He says you were sensational in your new picture, *As Far As the Heart Can Tell* ...'

'Perhaps that should be my next picture,' said Meg. 'This one is *As Far As the Eye Can See*.'

After apologising, the editor went on: 'Joe's judgment is always spot on. We're thinking about reprising our Swinging London feature with you on the cover.'

'Wonderful,' said Lucy when she heard the news. 'You're the new Georgy Girl *, the next Julie Christie *.'

The photographer shot Meg in a variety of iconic locations: Westminster Abbey, the Tower of London, Big Ben, Carnaby Street *, cycling along King's Road Chelsea *, cruising along the Thames in a launch, riding on the platform of a double-deck bus, peering from a red phone box, leaping over railings (low) in Green Park, feeding the ducks in St James' Park.

'You're a wonderful subject,' the photographer told her. 'I don't have to keep asking you to smile. And your hair blows all over the place.'

'That's good?'

'That's very good. It says high spirits. That's the mood we want.'

Two days later the Time editor phoned again. 'The pictures are fantastic,' he enthused. 'I'm delighted. London's the place and you're the person. Meg, you're the personification of young London!'

# ELEVEN

THE French thought so too. 'It's you they want,' Walter Greening told Meg. 'They want you to get over there and really push the picture for them.'

The director and his two stars were gathered in the studio head's office. Greening explained that the French-language rights had been sold. *As Far As the Eye Can See* would be sub-titled and given a major release.

'What on earth do they want with our funny little picture? Haven't they got enough crap of their own?' said Bert Brump.

'Bert, this world-weary veteran bit can be overdone,' Greening responded only half in jest. 'You know it's a good picture. I'm pleased that the French have recognised that. I suppose they think it captures the spirit of London like *Breathless* * captured the spirit of Paris.'

Bert looked blank. Meg also struggled with the reference although the information was buried somewhere in her memory.

'I thought the scene where Jean Seberg sells the Herald-Tribune on the Champs Elysees was terribly good,' Bob Curzon supplied. It was a graceful way of filling in the blank of the others' ignorance.

'We could add a scene with Meg selling the Mirror in front of Buckingham Palace, I suppose,' said Bert. 'Until she gets moved on by some officious policeman,' he couldn't resist adding.

Greening ignored him. 'Quite so, Bob,' he said. 'I want

79

you there too. So, all of you, get over to Paris and do your best. You too, Bert. I can't not send you, can I? But please be on your best behaviour!'

Privately, Greening was as surprised as Bert that the French wanted the film. It was seen as conveyor belt fare to which little money had been allocated for publicity. The studio would send the three of them plus a publicity girl for just one night. But, as was inevitable, the stars and the director would stay at a first-rank hotel. Swallowing hard, Greening booked the publicity girl there also.

'These French journalists make me nervous,' Bert grumbled. He and Meg and publicity girls from both London and Paris were at the press conference in the George V hotel.

'I don't know why,' said Meg. 'We have an interpreter – and the questions will probably be in English.' Sure enough, the first one was.

'Mr Brump, what do you think this film has to offer French audiences?' said a young man in flawless English.

'I've no idea,' the director responded. 'You asked for it.'

The young man frowned in puzzlement. '"You asked for it". Doesn't that mean something nasty is going to happen to you?'

'Sometimes it does and sometimes it doesn't. In this case it simply means that the distributors here asked to show this picture.'

At this the whole room of twenty or so journalists looked puzzled. Into the silence Meg offered in fluent French: '*Vous le lui avez demandé* c'est une expression qui signifie que vous n'avez que ce que vous méritez, mais il a aussi un sens littéral que vous avez demandé quelque chose. Comme l'a dit Bert.'[*You asked for it* is an idiom meaning you deserve something bad to happen to you, but it also has a literal meaning that you have requested something. As Bert said]

The atmosphere in the room was transformed. Reporters and critics who had been staring morosely at the publicity material or scribbling half-heartedly in their notebooks became wide awake.

'Votre français est magnifique!' [Your French is magnificent!] someone exclaimed. Meg saw several others nodding in agreement.

'Comment avez-vous appris un si bon français?' [How did you learn such good French?]

'J'étais à l'école en Suisse,'[I was at school in Switzerland] Meg replied. 'Ah, ce qui explique l'accent!' [Ah, that explains the accent!] Everyone laughed.

'D'où je viens, vous êtes celui qui a un accent,' [Where I come from you're the one with the accent] Meg riposted. Everyone laughed even more loudly. She realised that she had the group with her. Pressing her advantage, she went on: 'Nous sommes honorés à l'occasion de montrer cette image en France – aren't we, Bert? Londres est un endroit passionnant de nos jours, et nous espérons que cette histoire d'une fille ordinaire qui gagne le cœur d'un millionnaire déguisé capture l'esprit de Londres.' [We are honoured at the chance of showing this picture in France. London is an exciting place these days, and we hope this tale of an ordinary girl who wins the heart of a millionaire in disguise captures the spirit of London]

'Mais vous n'êtes pas une fille ordinaire, milady,' [But

you aren't an ordinary girl, my lady] a cynic put in.

'Non, je suis une actrice,' [No, I'm an actress] Meg shot back. More laughter.

Bert, who had no idea what was said, looked displeased that Meg seemed to be turning into a comedienne.

'Perhaps we should get back to the picture,' said one of the publicity girls. 'Do you want to hear about the great locations we used in the film?' Silence. It seemed they didn't.

'Mr Brump, what does the English title, *As Far As the Eye Can See*, refer to?' asked an earnest girl with thick black glasses. 'And what do you think of the French title, *Le secret d'un veuf [A Widower's Secret]*?'

'I don't know what either of them mean,' the director replied. Laughter. 'Perhaps they both have a certain je ne sais quoi, whatever the French is for that [he added to the interpreter].' More laughter, Bert wasn't sure why.

'Bob here will be able to help us,' he added hastily.

'Excusez-moi si je parle en mauvais français,' [Excuse me if I speak in bad French] Bob began. 'Je ne peux pas égaler Meg en français.' [I can't equal Meg in French] His effort was greeted with nods of approval as he continued haltingly: '*As Far As the Eye Can See* est un jeu de mots. Les anglais aiment les calembours.' [*As Far As the Eye Can See* is a play on words. The English like puns] Nods of agreement. 'Comme une expression signifie la phrase autant que l'on peut imaginer. Donc, le personnage de Meg pense que je suis un homme ordinaire qui ne peut se permettre qu'un petit appartement. Il s'avère que je suis un millionnaire qui achète une maison de campagne avec terrain qui s'étend – littéralement

– pour autant que l'œil puisse voir.' [As an idiom the expression means as far as anyone knows. So Meg's character thinks I'm an ordinary man who can only afford a small apartment. It turns out that I'm a millionaire who buys a country estate with land stretching – literally – as far as the eye can see]

'Le titre français, *Le secret d'un veuf*, est très différent. Ne devrait-il pas être le même?' [The French title, *A Widower's Secret*, is very different. Shouldn't it be the same?] the earnest girl pursued.

'Titles are often different,' said the London publicity girl after the question had been translated. 'It's a matter of what's right for each market.'

The critic from Cahiers du film asked the director in English: 'M Brump, what are you trying to say in this picture?'

'I'm not trying to *say* anything. What I'm trying to *do* is tell a rattling good yarn.'

The interpreter struggled with this very English expression. Eventually she managed: 'Une histoire passionnante.'

The Cahiers critic looked dissatisfied. Meanwhile, a reporter from a mass-circulation newspaper thought the press conference should come back to earth.

'Est-ce que vous allez vous marier avec Everard Hughes?' [Are you going to marry Everard Hughes?] Meg was asked.

'Nous sommes très heureux ainsi.' [We're very happy as we are]

'Le studio est-il inquièt de l'effet sur vos fans quand vous, comme disent les Anglais, *live in sin*?' [Is the studio worried about the effect on your fans when you, as the English say, *live in sin*?] the reporter persisted.

'Le studio est cool avec ça,' [The studio is cool with it] she fibbed. 'Et il y a des péchés pires – ils me disent.' [And there are worse sins – so they tell me] Laughter.

They had a couple of hours to spare before the premiere that evening. Bob and Meg took the metro to Montmartre. They climbed the steps to the Sacre Cœur basilica and gazed over the rooftops of Paris. The uniform roofline was so sharply different from London's, which even then was being broken up into unplanned bits and pieces of different heights.

'What is it that gives Paris that special feeling?' Meg asked more to herself than to Bob. 'Is it the formality of the buildings and the grandeur of the streets contrasted with the friendly scale of the pavement cafes and small shops?'

'Perhaps it's better not to analyse it; just to enjoy it,' said Bob.

They skipped the basilica, preferring to have a coffee at a cafe in one of the small, ancient streets close by.

'It's the calm before the storm,' said Meg.

They needn't have worried. The audience at the Paris premiere laughed appreciatively as the London audience had done. In different places. They laughed when Meg's estate agent character offered her buyer a cup of coffee and produced a jar of Nescafe.

'That wasn't a funny bit,' Bert whispered to Meg.

'It is now,' she replied.

They laughed when, towards the end of the picture, she showed her buyer the country mansion where they would live happily ever afterwards. Bob Curzon delivered the widower's line with nonchalance as he took in the magnificent estate stretching as far as the eye could see: 'I think this will do.'

Bert dug Meg in the ribs and looked quizzical.

'I expect it sounds very English to them,' she said.

'Who cares as long as they put their French backsides on the seats,' the director replied.

'Congratulations, everybody,' said Bert as they sat in the hotel after the show. 'I don't know how we did it but we did. That obviously went really well.'

The publicity girl said: 'I must phone my boyfriend. Then I'm turning in. Goodnight, all.'

'It's been a long day for a middle-aged bloke like me. I'm for bed too,' said Bert.

'Whose bed?' asked Bob when the director had gone. 'Do you think he wants to make out with her?'

'I expect so,' said Meg. 'But he won't get anywhere.'

'The night's still young. Let's go out,' said Bob.

'Get thee behind me, Satan!' Meg laughed.

'If I was Satan I'd suggest we stay in.'

'Naughty!' said Meg, giving him a playful slap.

As they wandered the streets at random, Bob asked: 'May I hold your hand?'

'You're very coy all of a sudden, Mr Curzon,' she answered as she took his hand.

'It's a long time since I spent a month in bed with you – even if the director and a large crew were watching.'

They came to a club from whose open doors a woman's singing could be heard. The song was mournful but melodic – an irresistible invitation to dance.

'Bonjour Tristesse, *' said Meg. 'Can it really be Juliette Greco singing?'

'Either way, this is for us,' said Bob.

'Je suis désolé, monsieur. Le club est réservée aux membres,' [I'm sorry, monsieur. The club is for members only] said the doorman, blocking their way.

'Nous sommes des visiteurs venus d'Angleterre, ici pour une nuit seulement,' [We are visitors from England, here for one night only] said Meg in her most winning manner.

The doorman shrugged and said nothing.

'Cette dame est une grande star de cinéma en Angleterre - et partout dans le monde, bien sûr,' [This lady is a big film star in England – and all over the world, of course] said Bob. 'Nous aimerions une adhésion temporaire à votre club.' [We would like a temporary membership of your club]

'Monsieur,' said the doorman, 'nous avons beaucoup de stars de cinéma dans ce club. Et membre temporaire n'est pas possible.' [We have many film stars at this club. And temporary membership isn't possible]

Bob wasn't beaten yet. 'Nous sommes ici pour la première du nouveau film de Miss Meg Denby avec notre directeur, Bert Brump. Le film sera un grand succès en France.' [We are here for the premiere of Miss Meg Denby's new film with our director, Bert Brump. The film will be a big hit in France]

The doorman's bored obduracy gave way to animated interest. 'Vous dites Bert Brump? Un nouveau film de M. Brump? Ses films sont comme votre Carry On série, je suis un grand fan. Oh oui, presque aussi bon que le Carry On films.' [You say Bert Brump? A new film by M. Brump? His films are like your Carry On * series I'm a big fan. Oh yes, almost as good as the Carry On films]

They were in. The singer wasn't Juliette Greco, but she was just as fine.

They got back to the hotel at 3am, weary but happy. Once again they stood in a hotel corridor with the building encased in deepest night. Memories of Great Torrington. Their rooms were next to each other.

'Plane early tomorrow ... I mean this morning!' said Bob.

Meg looked at him questioningly.

'Good night, milady,' he said softly.

She said nothing as he enfolded her in his arms; then she eased her head on to his shoulder.

'You're gorgeous, Meg. You're everything a man can want but you're not mine. I'm very committed to Meryl.'

She was choked with emotion. 'But Torrington ...' she managed.

'Torrington was very special. I'll remember it to the end of my days,' said Bob. 'But it can never be repeated. It would never be as good again, so why should we try? We must keep it as our own, our very own beautiful memory.'

He released his hold on her. 'Good night', he said again, and was gone.

The French press reviews for *Le secret d'un veuf* were uniformly favourable. All agreed that it was more than a simple tale of a working girl who sells an ordinary flat to a millionaire in disguise – and wins his heart through her energy and commitment.

'This is at bottom a disquisition on social fluency and democracy,' declared one newspaper. 'The spirit of young London isn't confined to the rich and well connected. The miniskirt is available to all.'

Another newspaper discovered the opposite: 'The plot is trite, no doubt deliberately so, but this apparent comedy is really about the English social order. In stratified England even today a rich man has to disguise himself to find someone who will love him for himself and not his money.'

The theme was echoed by a Marxist magazine, which described the film as 'a subtle and well directed attack on the English class system where estates of the size depicted continue to exist, and the only way an ordinary person can share in them is by accident'.

The magazine represented by the girl with the black glasses said *Le secret d'un veuf* 'helps us understand the English obsession with class, which France left behind in the 18th century'.

The same magazine praised Meg not for what she did but for what she was. 'Meg Denby is beautiful, but this is clearly nothing to the purpose of director Bert Brump. She is an aristocrat in real life, playing a working girl who ends as an aristocrat by accident – a trenchant statement about the nature of chance.'

Cahiers du film praised the film as 'seminal'. It said: 'This is a richly layered picture with meta-narratives well worth the effort of unpicking. Director Bert Brump is an ironist of the first order. He represents himself as a journeyman film-maker (he was at his ironical best at a recent press conference pretending to have all the social skills of a bricklayer), but he is in reality an auteur with much to tell us about human relations through the prism of class and the role of fate in human affairs. The film's philosophical underpinnings place it in the Berkeleyan mould on the nature of reality.'

'I don't know what you did over there but it worked,' said Walter Greening when they met again in his office.

'And to think that I never knew what I was making!' said Bert.

'Are you joking again?' Greening asked.

# TWELVE

HOLLYWOOD came calling for Meg in the form of Harold Cohen, the talent scout who approached her at the premiere of *As Far As the Eye Can See*. He confirmed that Monumental Pictures wanted to see her, and followed this with an air ticket for Los Angeles.

'There's a big budget Tudor historical epic they want you to test for,' he explained.

She left it to Ken, her agent, to obtain clearance from her British studio. Fortunately her contract allowed her to take a time-out before making her next picture. It wasn't to be that simple, however. She was summoned to see the head of the studio.

'This is a great opportunity for you, Meg,' said Walter Greening. 'But you want to go next week for a month in the first instance. That makes things very tricky for us. As you know, we're lined up to start shooting your picture at that time. It will be too expensive to stand everyone down.'

'When Hollywood calls it's difficult to say no, Mr Greening,' Meg urged.

'No one wants you to say no ... of course not. But if you could put them off for, say, a month we can make a start here and then shoot around you while you're away.'

'My contract says I can take a break ...'

'It also says that the break must be upon due notice.'

Ken the agent had considered this and convinced himself that the contract was ambiguous on the point.

'Mr Greening, I'm very sorry, but my agent says that I can't afford not to go when they want me. He says the contract side is OK.'

Greening sighed with the weariness of a man who was tired of being a way-station for Hollywood.

'Meg, our business is all about balancing professional obligations,' he observed. 'I can't physically lock the door and stop you going, but please have another think.'

But she knew she wouldn't.

Meg was unprepared for the scale of America – the wide avenues and boulevards of Los Angeles, the huge cars, the sense that the city sprawled forever, the pervasive smog now vanished from London after the Clean Air Act *. The shopping malls with their massive parking lots, where people drove to find giant stores congregating in the middle of nowhere, were utterly new to her. She thought of the narrow streets and small family businesses of Ripon, but London too had nothing like these malls.

The house they had assigned Everard was gorgeous – a spacious bungalow with picture windows running the full length of the living room. A profusion of bourgainvillea covered the outside walls. The patio beyond gave an uninterrupted view of the Pacific Ocean, bathed now in the red light of the setting sun.

'It's breathtaking,' she murmured.

It was just as he had promised her that night at Lowmere. He'd even remembered the orange juice, which, with ice and beyond doubt freshly squeezed, was set on a table awaiting her.

A young man came forward. He was of lean build and middle height. He was a year or two younger than her,

Meg guessed. Her chief impression was of hair. He had a luxuriant moustache and long, black hair.

'This is Jason,' said Everard, 'who shares with me. I'd have been lost in the early days without him showing me round LA.'

'Hi,' said Jason, although not with quite the usual enthusiasm that Americans put into an initial greeting.'

'Hi,' said Meg, but the word sounded strange to her as she said it. 'What a wonderful place you have here.'

It was Everard who answered. 'It's in the studio's top rental band. I'm lucky.' He managed to suggest that it was nothing more than he deserved.

'You must be tired after your flight,' said Jason. 'Let me take your bags and show you your room.'

The bedroom contained a huge double bed and, being next to the living room, enjoyed the same glorious view of the ocean.

'I can just see myself sitting in bed and enjoying the sunrise over the ocean,' Meg enthused.

Meg had found out from Everard that Jason would be staying on. She was conscious that she was the third person in what had been a successful two-person houseshare. She knew this because Ev had said so in his phone calls.

She wanted to reassure Jason, who might be nervous on the point, that this was fine with her. 'I'm sure we'll all get on well together,' she said as they sat over a supper prepared by Jason.

It turned out that he worked as a technician at Monumental Pictures. He was from Akron, Ohio – 'the typical sort of place that people come to Hollywood from,' he said in a departure from his usual style of short, factual answers. He was very quiet around Meg, usually waiting for her to speak first. She felt sure that would change as he got to know her better.

Everard's love-making that night was unusually lacklustre. He struggled to achieve any sort of an erection.

'I'm tired,' he said.

'It doesn't matter at all,' said Meg, meaning it. She snuggled into the curve of his long frame. 'But shouldn't I be the one to be tired?'

After the hiccup of the first night, their love-making reached new heights in the sunshine of California. They switched off the air-conditioning, opened the windows and enjoyed the distant sounds of the city. Jason in the next room was forgotten. Meg often took the initiative and found Everard always ready. She liked to tickle the underside of his balls, whereupon his apparatus elevated itself with the inevitability of an automatic door. She took him into her mouth greedily.

As the days went by, Meg saw little of Jason and (except at night) not much more of Everard. They were all so busy on their different activities. But when they encountered each other, Meg felt a constraint in Jason; a tenseness in her presence. He never used her name.

Eventually she was driven to say: 'Jason, we don't seem to talk much. Have I done something to offend you?'

He didn't look up. He was stacking the fridge at the time. In went the bread, the jam, both boxes of breakfast cereal, instant coffee in a glass jar. She hadn't got used to the American habit of putting everything into their huge refrigerators.

'Nothing at all,' he replied. 'It's just my way.'

Meg soon found herself before the president and chief executive of Monumental Pictures, Solly Michaels. His office lived up to the name of his company. At the far end could be discerned a bald man smoking a cigar. When he stood up, she wasn't surprised that he was short. He was the very template of the movie mogul.

'Welcome to Hollywood ... welcome to America, Miss Danby,' he enthused. 'I hear you've been a knockout in your new movie, *As Far As Anyone Knows*,' he went on. 'I have the box office. Sensational! We'll be distributing it here. You'll be a name in no time.'

Meg didn't mind being 'Miss Danby' but she felt she must correct him about the name of the film. 'Excuse me, Mr Michaels, but my picture is *As Far As the Eye Can See*.'

'Yes, yes,' he responded, as if the title was a trivial detail to be ignored. 'We see you as [looking at papers on his desk] Elizabeth of York in a Tudor epic. We'll call it *A Multicolored Rose*. You know why we call it that?'

As it happens, Meg did but she judged it wise to pretend ignorance. She opened her eyes to their widest. 'No, why, Mr Michaels?'

'Because by marrying Henry VIII she united two warring families both claiming the English throne, like Romeo and Juliet but with a happy ending. Liz was young and beautiful. Like you, my dear. She went on to have six lovely kids with him. Or did he have six wives? Never mind – although if he did we'll have to play down that bit.

'You'll be perfect as Liz – subject to a screen test, of course. The picture will be sensational. The 18th century was an era of chivalry and romance and deeds of valour. You'll fit right in, believe me!'

Meg hoped that the writers for *A Multicolored Rose* had a firmer grasp of history than Mr Michaels. But she couldn't help liking him and his exuberance. Underneath, she judged him to be a kind man.

'Settling in all right?' he said. 'Accommodations satisfactory? If you have any problems, let my assistant Miss Street know. She'll soon fix them for you. And you must come and have dinner soon.' Aware of the construction this might bear, he added: 'With my wife and me at our home. Bring your hmmm friend, Everest ...?'

'*Everard* Hughes, Mr Michaels.'

'Of course, Miss Danby, of course. He's one of our contract players, isn't he?'

Meg took her screen test, in which she was lighted and shot from every imaginable angle. She was asked to deliver chunks of text representing a heroine character in a variety of moods. The excerpts were obviously from *A Multicolored Rose*. She was relieved to find that the material was both sensitive and accurate.

She then waited for days during which she heard nothing from the studio. Twice she went to see Miss Street, to be assured that 'everything is in the works'. Nor was there any dinner invitation from Mr Michaels.

Bob Supple was to be a co-star on the planned picture. One day at the studio Meg noticed the imitation dog-tags with peace symbols around his neck. Seeing where she was looking, he said simply: 'Vietnam. Replicas, of course. To show support for peace.'

'I know,' she replied. 'I'm pretty active in the peace movement in Britain.'

'Wow, that's cool! There's a march in town next week. Would you care to come?'

She said yes, provided the studio didn't need her. They arranged a meeting point and a time. She found the place without difficulty. Thousands of peaceniks were gathering and preparing to march on City Hall.

The noise was overwhelming as chants and songs cancelled each other out. One slogan, the most repeated of all, could be made out above the wall of noise: 'Hey, hey, LBJ, how many kids did you kill today?'

They filled the streets to a depth of several blocks. Ranks of police were to be seen. Mounted officers moved along the edges of the crowd, penning the protesters within whatever limits they had decreed.

The agreed meeting time came and went – but where was Bob Supple? She realised then that, for whatever reason, Bob wasn't coming. The last of the marchers were now moving towards City Hall. Meg attached herself loosely to a small group, mainly women, and moved with them.

A young man with a camera stood in her path. Straining to be heard over the chanting and singing and shrieks of good-natured laughter around them, he said: 'Pardon me, miss. Los Angeles Times. We're taking pictures for our coverage. May I know your name please.'

Picking up on her accent, he shouted: 'Are you a visitor?'

'I'm here to work, as a matter of fact.'

'And what work is that, Meg?'

'I'm an actress.'

'One of thousands in this town,' he said. 'I hope it works out for you.'

She got home that evening to find Everard and Jason laughing and enjoying drinks on the sun-drenched patio. The mood changed immediately as she appeared. Everard started to berate her for joining the march.

'You're not in England now,' he said. 'These people [whoever "these people" were] are sensitive about Vietnam. You shouldn't have done it, Meg.'

It's nothing to do with me being a foreigner,' Meg objected. 'Vietnam affects everyone in the world. I have the right to protest.'

Jason said nothing and tried to look as if he wasn't there.

'What do you think, Jason?' she said, hoping he would support her.

'You must do whatever you think right' was all he would say.

'You may have the right, but Monumental will hate the publicity,' Everard persisted. 'It could destroy your career here before it's started.'

'I don't see what it's to do with Monumental. I'm only doing what thousands of others are doing,' said Meg. 'America says it's the home of free speech so they above all must understand that young people want to be heard.'

'Free speech is only the theory. The bosses here don't go around with a copy of the constitution in their pockets,' said Everard.

Meg shot back: 'Don't be absurd! Everyone knows about the right of free speech. Look, Ev, I'm glad I did it – and I'll do it again. I went as a marcher, not a speaker. There will be no publicity.'

In this she was wrong. The next day's LA Times ran a large picture of her at the march, with the caption: 'Actress Meg Denby from England was one of the protesters.' They had highlighted her from all the pictures the photographer took that day.

The next day Time rang from London. 'You spoke at the Vietnam rally in Hyde Park a few weeks ago,' the editor said.

Meg agreed that she had.

'And you were on yesterday's march in Los Angeles.' He had obviously seen the LA Times. 'It seems you're very active in the peace movement, so called.'

He wasn't asking questions, but making statements that were obviously leading up to something; almost certainly nothing good.

'Vietnam is the most important issue of our time,' she said. 'On both sides of the Atlantic,' she couldn't resist adding.

'Maybe, maybe not,' said the editor. 'Many of our readers – probably most – disagree with you. American lives are being lost in Vietnam. Readers feel strongly about the protests and the draft-dodging to Canada and Sweden that these protests encourage.

'Our readers don't want to see people like you in the magazine. I'm sorry, Miss Denby. Our Swinging London feature is going ahead, but you won't be in it.'

# THIRTEEN

THE Hollywood Scribe was a magazine second only to Variety in its impact with the film community. It was a clever mix of gossip and solid insider information – essential reading from the moguls to the newest production assistant. Soon after the peace march this item appeared:

### ARISTO MEG SPEAKS OUT ON VIETNAM

English import the Honourable Meg Denby, slated for Elizabeth of York in Monumental's forthcoming *A Multicolored Rose*, is of a very different stripe than her politician father. Aristocratic Lord Chilcott is an active supporter of America's effort in Vietnam, but his disobedient daughter is a leading light of the peace movement.

Militant Meg has pounded the London streets handing out leaflets, and she was a keynote speaker at a mass rally in the city's Hyde Park. Here in LA she joined in last week's march on City Hall.

'Our enemy is the small group of evil people behind this war – the US military-industrial complex,' the Hon Meg told the Hyde Park protesters. Working herself into a lather, she declared: 'They want this war and they profit from this war. But we can beat these evil people and we can end this war … we can overcome!'

> Unmarried Meg has a love-child with Everard Hughes, also a Monumental player, with whom she's living in Los Angeles. But the beauteous star isn't above a fling with other thesps. On location for her hit English movie *As Far As I'm Concerned* the frisky filly canoodled with her co-star, married Bob Curzon, before disappearing together into the night.
>
> Quite a gal, who's sure to get plenty of publicity for Monumental!

The article was illustrated with shots of Meg in Hyde Park, handing out leaflets at Kings Cross, in the kebab shop with Bob Curzon at Great Torrington and on the march to City Hall. For most of the Scribe's readers, it was one more piece of spicy tittle-tattle, but for Meg the effect of this well informed hatchet job was devastating.

Everard stormed into the living room waving a copy of Hollywood Scribe. 'Bitch!' he said, hitting her on the cheek.

'Ev, I'm so sorry ...'

'And how many others while I've been away, I wonder.'

'No others, I swear, Ev.'

'Can't think why I should believe you,' he said, and stormed out again.

Solly Michaels was more polite, but the president of Monumental Pictures was also very angry.

'How could you do this to me, Miss Danby?' he said.

'I'm so sorry, Mr Michaels. I didn't ask to be photographed. He just sprang it on me. I don't know how they got hold of the pictures from Britain.'

'Our sins usually find us out sooner or later. You may think Vietnam is a simple issue, but here in America it isn't. Boys are dying over there. Families are divided. We don't want people looking at our star and saying "That's the horrible girl who supports the Commies. I'm not going to watch a movie with her in it". That's bad for the box office and bad for Monumental's reputation.'

It was Walter Greening's objection over again.

'I can only apologise ...'

Ignoring the apology, Michaels said: 'Now about the other matter, is it true that you have a child without having been married?'

'Yes, but I was almost married . He left me at the last moment before the wedding. When I was setting out for the church, in fact.'

Michaels looked startled. 'Why would er- er-Hughes want to leave a lovely young woman like you? He should count himself lucky to have you as his bride.'

'It wasn't Everard, Mr Michaels.'

The mogul was bemused. The complications of young people's love lives were quite beyond him. The more beautiful the people, the more complicated their lives seemed to be. And Monumental had its full share of beautiful people.

Meg explained that she found she was pregnant with Everard's baby and he didn't want to get married; but she knew that one should be married before having a baby and another person – very unsuitable really – was there and – then she burst into tears.

Michaels' reaction was to call for his assistant. Miss Street hugged the younger woman consolingly and helped her to compose herself; then, job done, she left the room and the mogul resumed his interrogation..

'So if you're well enough, Miss Danby, I believe I ought to continue. I understand that you're living openly with Hughes here in Los Angeles.'

Meg agreed that she was.

'And while you were on location for your movie *As Far As That Goes* you had an affair with your co-star, who is a married man.'

'It wasn't an affair, Mr Michaels. It only happened once. We were celebrating the end of the shoot, and we got carried away.'

The mogul sighed. 'All these things are problems for Monumental,' he said. 'We make family pictures. We have to insist that our talent maintain wholesome reputations.'

He paused in embarrassment before passing sentence.

'I'm sorry, Miss Danby – Meg – in many respects you are clearly a fine person. I have good reports of your willingness to work and your punctuality; how well you get along with the rest of the cast and crew. You're the sort of person we like to have on our team – but for the sake of the studio I can't be seen to condone moral turpitude of any kind. We can't take up our option for you to star in *A Multicolored Rose*.'

She reached the commissary before she broke up into tears again. The others in the room, fearing to get sucked into a difficult situation, ignored her until she was found by Tom Supple.

'Gee, I feel horrible about this. I got you into it,' he said after she had told him how her Hollywood dream had collapsed.

'Where were you on the march?' she asked. 'You weren't at the meeting point. I waited.'

'I didn't make it to the march. There were special reasons. I knew it would damage my career if it came out.'

'And you never bothered to warn me?' Meg asked incredulously.

'I tried, really I did. I'd lost your number, and nobody else had it. I even went to your house, but you'd left for the march already.'

Tom explained that he'd been tipped off that the FBI would be crawling all over the event, targeting names and faces recognisable to the public with the intention of discrediting them.

'That's how they work,' he said. 'They get what they think is something on someone, and then they plant it in the press as black propaganda. Journalists are suckers. They convince themselves they have hot exclusives. The photographer who took your picture was probably an agent himself. He didn't find you by chance among all those thousands.'

'Why me? And how did they get those pictures from England?'

'Because you are a potential role model for young women, but one who undermined the Great American War Effort by speaking out. And the pictures would have come from your security people, MI5. They have the closest possible links – shared values in support of our two great nations, and all that crap.'

'Daddy warned me and I didn't believe him,' said Meg.

'You should believe everything about those bastards,' said Bob. 'Watch out for yourself, Meg. They're out to get you.'

# FOURTEEN

EVERARD, whom she had always accepted as the most self-centred of people, showed unsuspected depths of sympathy. The Hollywood Scribe episode forgotten, he insisted on joining her on the long, miserable flight home, and he was at her side for the impromptu press conference at Heathrow Airport. Meg's dismissal from the picture had been all over the London papers. Photographers and reporters were waiting for her in flight arrivals.

'Better to get it out of the way now,' he counselled. 'The press won't want to do it again later.'

'Miss Denby ...' Someone from the pack had to be first. 'How are you feeling?'

'Jet-lagged – and looking forward to getting home,' Meg replied.

'And sad?'

'Sad, naturally.'

'Tell us what happened, Meg.'

'They decided I wasn't right in the part after all. I respect that decision, and I'm grateful for my experiences in Hollywood.'

'Do you hope ...

'The buzz is ...'

'Hey, guys and guyesses, one at a time please,' Everard broke in.

'The buzz is,' said a woman who was quickest on the draw, 'that you were fired because of your involvement with the peace movement.'

'Absolutely not. It was an artistic judgment by the studio.'

'Do you think British security put the Americans up to it?'

'I already said it was nothing to do with Vietnam so the question can't apply,' Meg answered mildly. No point in riling them even though the reporter was on a fishing expedition.

'Will you continue to work with the peace movement?'

'Vietnam isn't the issue here – but naturally I'll keep doing what I can for peace.'

'What are your plans now, Meg?'

'To relax – with Everard [she squeezed his hand; he responded with an adoring look] – and then get back to work. There's plenty for me here in Britain.'

'Would you like to go back to Hollywood?'

'If they want me, they know where I am.'

'Everard, are you returning to Hollywood?'

'When Meg can spare me [he shot her another adoring look] I have to go back to finish a picture.'

'Thank you, all,' said Meg.

They started to move towards the taxi rank. The press pack dropped away one by one while curious bystanders looked on.

'Can I give you a lift home?' said a famous buy-up merchant. He saw a fantastic exclusive account if he could only land it. But the offer was declined.

'I'm sure that put them off the scent,' said Everard in the taxi.

'I hate to lie like that,' Meg observed.

'That's how the game is played, sweetheart. We have to support the studio line on why you were let go.'

The road into London appeared crowded and cramped compared with the spacious avenues and boulevards of Los Angeles. It was a typical dismal day. Even the miniskirted girls didn't add much gaiety to the scene.

Her flat was exactly as Meg had left it a month ago. The final breakfast things, which she hadn't had time to wash up, were in the sink. Her plants, which she had forgotten to leave with a neighbour, were drooping and possibly dead. The flat itself seemed small and cheerless.

'What a homecoming!' Meg collapsed on the bed and sobbed. Everard lay down beside her. He didn't come on to her, sensing that she needed only quietness and the feeling of him beside her. They stayed that way for hours.

Eventually, the old Ev reasserted itself and he announced he was going out. He didn't say where. 'Just some fresh air,' he said.

The answer machine had messages of support from Lucy, Haverstock, Ken the agent and many others. She would have to respond to them, but not right now. And she must get out of London for a time. Everywhere she went in the city people would want to talk about what happened in Hollywood. She must leave until the fuss died down. She would go to Lowmere and Ben.

Next morning a composed Meg asked Everard about his plans. He evidently judged her cured, or cured enough, and said he had to get back to California. Soon he was gone.

Lowmere was its unchanging self, serene in the spring sunshine. In the nursery, however, things had gone from bad to worse. Ben appeared not to recognise her, or if he did was as indifferent to her as to any other kindly stranger.

Pointing to a rubber ball, he announced, 'Palla!' He then indicated a Lego house and declared, 'Casa!' Now there was no doubt. Meg complained furiously to Julia about Ben speaking Italian. The girl insisted she had no idea where he got these words. It was useless. The only solution was for the nanny to go.

'How could you let Julia speak to Ben in Italian?' Meg demanded of her mother.

'I expect she uses English as well, darling,' said Lady Chilcott. 'I'm sure Ben will grow out of his Italian when he leaves the nursery. And don't you think it's better for Ben to learn Italian rather than English with an Italian accent? That was your grandparents' view in India when they insisted that the native servants spoke Hindi to your father.'

Lady Chilcott produced her trump card: 'It hasn't done Daddy any harm, has it?'

Meg protested: 'I don't want Ben growing up confused. I think Julia should be replaced.'

Lady Chilcott observed that dependable nannies were hard to find, and these days they were mostly foreigners of one sort or another in any case. 'If you're that unhappy, darling, you'll have to look after Ben yourself,' she added.

'Mummy, I may have to start doing that despite my work and everything.' Even as she said it Meg knew it couldn't happen. She wouldn't know where to begin. She told herself Ben would be happier growing up in the spacious setting of Lowmere than in her small flat.

Meg stayed at Lowmere for three weeks, recovering gradually from the trauma of Hollywood. Her parents were away much of the time on their frantic rounds of social and philanthropic commitments. She became used to having her meals in the small sitting room. She yearned for company, even Julia's and Ben's, but never got around to inviting them downstairs.

The tranquil days were punctuated only by frequent calls from Everard. He had become more solicitous since her Hollywood interlude. She heard nothing from her agent or the press. Even her peace group was getting along without her. She began to feel guilty about having done no campaigning since that march in LA. In every way, she was becoming the forgotten woman. It was time to return to London.

Meg sat in the studio boss's office, confident she could pick up her British career. She had sat in this office barely two months ago when she invoked the get-out clause in her contract. She had left the boss, Walter Greening, on reasonably good terms – not the best, but it had been far from storming out and slamming the door behind her.

'I'm sorry it didn't work out in LA,' Greening began.

'They felt I wasn't right in the part after all,' Meg explained.

Greening said nothing for a moment; made a show of examining papers on his desk. Then he smiled. 'You underestimate how much we studios talk to each other across the water. We know.'

'Know what?' Meg asked unwisely.

'That Monumental couldn't accept your political campaigning. The peace march in LA was the final straw. In advertising-speak, your activities "tarnish your image". Theirs too, by association.

'Look, Meg,' Greening went on, 'I'm old enough to be your father. You won't mind me making a fatherly observation, I'm sure. The same image thing applies in Britain. We're a tolerant lot, and we aren't as involved with blood and sweat in Vietnam as the Americans. Even so, you're doing your career no good with this politicking.

'You're the wholesome, girl next door type in your pictures (not that I'm suggesting you aren't in real life). Girls next door don't go on marches and rallies, much less speak at them.'

'Mr Greening, you sound like my father. He says the same. I can't bring myself to give up my peace work. Don't you think that young people, who are the ones fighting this war, have a duty to speak their minds about the war?'

Greening ignored the question, responding in a weary tone: 'At least I tried to tell you. But you wanted to see me, Meg.'

She explained that the experience in Hollywood had made her unwell, but she had now recovered. She had taken a time-out as her British contract allowed, and was ready to resume work.

'You'll understand that the film you couldn't make is now well into production,' said Greening. 'We cast Alison Adams in your place. She doesn't have your experience or your ability, at least not yet, but she has a marvellous freshness about her.'

Meg tried to persuade herself that the last comment wasn't a dig at her by comparison.

'Of course I understand the picture couldn't wait, Mr Greening. When do you expect to be able to offer me something else?

'We won't necessarily be able to offer you anything else. It depends on the right vehicle coming along.'

'But my contract ...'

Greening's mask slipped. Meg glimpsed an angry man. He picked up what was evidently her contract. 'You took a time-out as allowed under clause 5 A i. Contracts are often reciprocal. Clause 5 A ii is our entitlement. It provides that if you decline an offered picture for a reason other than medically attested illness, the studio may decline to offer further work under the contract at its judgment.

'As I say, it depends on the right vehicle coming along. I hope it does, Meg, but for the moment we have nothing for you.'

With difficulty she extricated herself from Greening's office with her composure intact. She gave way to tears, unseen, in a corridor. She had just recovered herself when Alison Adams came along. The girl was delighted to see her as usual, and expressed sympathy for what happened in Hollywood.

'That's how it is sometimes,' said Meg. 'It was an adventure.'

'I'm playing the role you couldn't do,' said Alison. 'That's an adventure for me. Of course, I'm not a patch on you, but they had to have someone. We're nearly finished actually. Oh, and I had to give up campaigning at Kings Cross. Mr Greening said it wasn't a good idea.'

Meg couldn't help liking the girl. She was as she Meg had been in her Haverstock years.

'What are you doing next?' Meg inquired.

Alison hesitated. Her bubbliness had disappeared. Then she settled for the truth: 'As a matter of fact, I had a call from Monumental Pictures. I'm going out to Hollywood next week for a screen test.'

At least Meg's advertisement for Tundra gin was

proving a big hit. Even then the advertiser was in no hurry to commission a follow-up.

# FIFTEEN

LONDON had ceased to swing for one unemployed actress. Money was not the problem. Her trust fund remained, even if the trustees doled out smaller amounts than Meg and her brothers Jeremy and Thomas would have liked. Her income became modest, but she had lost the urge to spend. It wasn't fun any more. She had long talks with Lucy, called frequently on Haverstock, stayed with Thomas at the Denby townhouse in Belgravia, had tea at the House of Commons with Jeremy, watched films. She tended to avoid parties and, in particular, fashion shows and clothes boutiques. Meg was bored. She knew she was drifting.

'It was the march on City Hall in LA that did it,' said Haverstock as they sat together in his flat. 'Hyde Park would have been an annoyance for the FBI, nothing more. The same thing on their own turf they were never going to let pass.'

'I can't have been that important to them,' said Meg wonderingly.

'Oh yes you were, potentially. It wasn't a chance they would take. Your American picture might have been a huge success. They saw you as a toxic model for the young. J. Edgar Hoover is a filthy little man * who has so much on everybody that he can't be fired.

'The FBI under Hoover has agents all over Hollywood. They'll "neutralise" anyone they dislike. You can take it for granted that the Scribe didn't come by that information by happy accident. It was planted. That's how they work.'

Haverstock took her into his arms in a gesture that was both intimate and passion-free. 'I'm worried about you, little star. The water has become too deep.'

'Is this the war hero speaking?'

'Even war heroes don't throw their lives away in battles they can't win. It's time to stop, Meg.'

She replied: 'You had your war; this is mine. And anyway, how much life have I got to throw away now?'

So she pounded the streets again, handing out anti-war pamphlets, speaking at rallies and marching here and there for peace. It all took organising. Meg became the lynchpin at the campaign's tiny office above a squalid betting shop in Kings Cross.

She pounded another set of streets for her new enthusiasm, women's liberation. The unofficial leader of the group that camped at Lowmere, a woman named Suze, welcomed her warmly, being glad of her name and her shoe leather.

'There's this woman Germaine something who has a book coming out called *The Female Eunuch* \*,' said Suze. 'It will be as big as Friedan. Title says it all. It shows what men will do to keep us in our place. They hate us because they're frightened of us.'

'I can't believe that my father and brothers secretly hate me,' said Meg.

'You've got a lot to learn,' Suze replied.

Meg found that campaigning, so important to her, wasn't enough anymore. She needed her career to focus and make sense of all her activities. She had always told herself that acting was a coat she could put on and take off as she pleased. When they had torn off her coat, she knew it wasn't so. She had become too used to being Meg Denby film star.

London was the same all around her, but she clearly wasn't. Pot no longer lifted her mood. She supposed she was depressed. Perhaps she should try the 'uppers' that several of her friends used. Really, however, Everard was the answer. With all she had lost, at least she had him. She ached for Ev, not mainly for the sex but for the comfort of his hand in hers, his body asleep next to her at four in the morning.

And suddenly he was with her, his work in Hollywood over for the foreseeable future.

Meg came out of the bathroom stark naked as Everard lay on the bed and admired the sight of her full frontal. Her long hair was hidden under a bathing cap, transforming her appearance. She followed his eyes as they traversed her body lingeringly from top to toe. She rejoiced that she could still excite him, one of the most sexually desirable men in London.

He stood up and made to move towards her. She read his intention. She could hardly not. The shape of his trousers told the story.

'Oh no, Ev, not now,' she said. 'It's four in the afternoon, I've just showered and I have to be out in ten minutes.'

He shook his head vigorously in mock anger.

'You're a real prick tease, Miss Denby, do you know that? ... Oh shit, now you've made me shake my stud off!'

Everard was proud of his ear stud, which he said made him look like a gipsy. He dropped to the ground searching for it.

'Oh Ev!' Meg said. She went on to her hands and

knees to help him. And he had clamped himself on to her from behind, his jeans and slip torn to his ankles. She felt a shaft of the most extreme pain as he found his way inside her with no preliminaries whatsoever.

'Dry sex,' he said matter-of-factly before getting down to work. 'Native peoples have always known about it. It increases the pleasure for both the man and the woman.'

It didn't seem that way to Meg at that moment. She felt she was about to cry in pain. And then the agony gave way to pleasure as her body, all resentment abandoned, began to respond to his rhythm. The pleasure seemed to be greater than usual, just as he had said, and soon she had lost herself in a stunning orgasm.

She tightened the vaginal muscles to clamp him harder. 'Oh yes please,' he said, sounding as lost in the occasion as she was.

Everard, famous for his staying power, was in no hurry to come. For Meg all sense of time and place had disappeared. Eventually awareness broke through and she began to feel that she'd had enough. It must have been the same for him. She felt his body tense and straighten, and both were swept up in huge simultaneous orgasms.

Meg returned to earth to find herself drenched in sweat. Somehow they had ended up in bed. She had no memory of getting there. Everard, equally wet, lay beside her, sated.

'Do it again please – but not too soon!' sighed Meg. Her appointment in ten minutes' time had been long forgotten.

Everard sat up in the bed, alert on the instant. 'There's no easy way to say this,' he began. 'There won't be any "again". I don't think it's right between us any more. Anyway, we haven't been together much lately, have we? [A long pause while Meg lay stupefied] There's someone else.'

It didn't make sense to her. 'What do you mean?' she asked stupidly.

'There's someone else I want to be with. I'm leaving, Meg. I'm sorry, I really am.'

Still she could say nothing. Everard blundered on: 'You'll find someone else. You're young, you're beautiful, you're famous, you're rich. You have a figure to die for ...'

She rallied at that. 'You bastard!' she said, dealing him a hard blow on the face. 'Don't patronise me.' The blow had cleared her head. 'Who is she?'

Everard hesitated again. 'Not she, he.'

She saw it in a flash. 'Jason?'

'Yes, Jason.'

So that was the explanation of Everard's 'housemate' when she came to Los Angeles, and the explanation for Jason's sulkiness when she moved in. The huge bedroom, with the big double bed and the view of the Pacific Ocean, was beyond doubt the room the men had shared. Jason had been pushed out to make way for her. Now she knew why Everard was disengaged in their acts of love, and why he often left this London flat without saying where he was going ... he was living the queer side of his life.

So Everard (she had already stopped thinking of him as 'Ev') was queer – but he also enjoyed women, as he had shown so many times. The horror was that she still wanted him. 'Jason's in Hollywood. We can be together when you're in London, can't we?'

She knew she was begging, and part of her hated herself for it.

'Jason's here in London,' he said. 'I've rented a flat for us.'

At that the tears finally came. Everard made no move to touch her. 'I'd better go,' he said. 'I'll send for my things.'

'Wait!' she said. 'Why, Everard, why? Half the women of the world are in love with you, and would give anything to be with you.'

'Women are too easy,' he said. 'I can turn all of you on like a light switch. There's no satisfaction in that. To arouse a man is harder. The challenge excites me.'

'Was it all a sham with me?'

'Not at all. I love you, Meg. A man can love another man and also a woman. Just not in the same way and not as much.'

'And that's it?'

'I never meant to deceive you, Meg, but I knew if I told you everything you wouldn't have stood for it. Thanks to you, no one thinks I'm queer. The truth is I needed you as a beard. But times have changed. I can come out – and keep my career.'

'You utter bastard!' She hit him on the cheek again.

She was both fully alive and still mesmerised by the violent love they had experienced. 'How were you able to make love to me so beautifully as you just did, feeling as you do?'

'I wanted to give you a special last experience to remember me by,' he said.

'You utter, utter bastard!'

This was the last she saw (disregarding him on screen) of Everard Hughes.

# SIXTEEN

AFTER crying herself senseless for twenty-four hours, hunger drove Meg out of the flat. The cupboard and the fridge were empty. And gradually, as the days crawled by, she accepted that she must do something to save herself. For a start, Ben needed her. No, that wasn't true. It was the thing people said about children and their mothers, but her son was clearly fine with Julia and, at a remove, Lady Chilcott. Perhaps when Ben was older he would need his mother, but not now; perhaps though she needed him.

For Meg at this lowest point there was only one place to be – Lowmere Abbey. The tranquil setting and the measured routine of life there eased her pain. The presence of Ben was a comfort even if she felt she had little to contribute to his life. The boy's Italian was coming along famously although his English was shaky.

Arnold Haverstock and Lucy Plessey were supportive. Lucy went firmly on to the front foot.

'You were too good for him,' she said.

'Then why did he dump me?' said Meg.

'You mean apart from being fucking queer? Because you're beautiful, intelligent, famous – and a lord's daughter. You've got everything, Meg, and men can't cope with that. They're pathetic!'

'Eeky, I don't have any luck with men,' said Meg, feeling sorry for herself. 'First Arnold, then that ludicrous episode with Howard Jenkins – my puppy dog, I called him – now Everard. They all walked out.'

'You've got Ben and I've got Rosie. That's all that matters. We don't need men. We need their sperm from time to time, but we don't need the bodies that go with it. The Seventies will be the decade of women, you see. At last we'll come into our own.'

In her misery, Meg found herself turning to the Vicar of Lowmere, the Reverend Hubert Atkinson. The old man had almost married her to Howard Jenkins. Since then she had avoided any but the most cursory encounters with him, feeling illogically that she was to blame for the ceremony not going ahead. Now she wanted to talk.

'Is it my fault that all my relationships end badly, Mr Atkinson?' she asked.

'As a woman you can hardly be blamed in the present – hmmm – circumstances,' he answered drily.

'Perhaps not, but before Everard there was Howard and before that Arnold Haverstock ...'

'Meg [he claimed the right to use her first name having christened her as a baby and watched her ever since], I don't pretend to know much about the modern world. In my day, one tended to marry the first girl one walked out with seriously. Even more so for the girls, I suppose. I do know, however, that it may be quite wrong to assume some underlying cause for three similar occurrences. The reason may be different in each case as it no doubt is here, my dear.

'In other words, it's not you. On the face of it, you've just been unlucky.'

'That's helpful, Mr Atkinson,' she said, 'but what do you mean "unlucky on the face of it"?'

'Meg, our Christian faith tells us that everything happens for a reason. Often it appears to be the opposite of what we want for ourselves. It's a test of faith. You have to believe, hard as it is,' he urged gently, his sincerity shining through, 'that these men weren't right for you, but that out there somewhere is one who is marked for you.'

She left the vicarage feeling comforted, but she wished she knew where to start looking.

Lord and Lady Chilcott did their best to help their daughter, but they had never really understood what drove her to eschew the traditional route for girls of her class and background. This was brief years of genteel work in London, perhaps in public relations, antiques, publishing or even estate agency, followed by marriage and life in the country. Even less did they understand her political commitment. Above all, they didn't understand Meg's feelings for Everard, whom they regarded as a worthless character; hence were unable to offer her much comfort in losing him.

Her brother Jeremy, the MP, thought grief was nonsense and she should just get on with it (whatever 'it' was). The other brother, Thomas, a more understanding character, tried to jolly her out of the blues.

'Plenty more where that came from,' he said. 'Roger Hudson for a start.'

Meg rolled her eyes in mock anguish. 'Can somebody please find Roger a wife? Then everyone will stop pressing me to marry him!'

She answered the phone one day as they were going in to dinner. With her mind elsewhere, she unwisely agreed that she was Meg Denby. The caller identified herself as from the Daily Mirror with 'a few questions'.

The reporter began in the recommended way with a

soft question. 'What are you doing these days?' she said.

'I'm considering several projects,' Meg lied. 'I hope something will be announced soon.'

'Can you be a bit more specific? Britain, America? Film, TV?'

'Not really at this point,' said Meg. The reporter let it go.

'How do you feel about the success of *As Far As the Eye Can See* in France?'

'I was thrilled'

'And a bit surprised?'

'A bit astonished, to be honest.'

'How do you feel about Everard Hughes leaving you for a man?'

The change of tone caught Meg off-guard. Eventually she managed: 'Everard and I are still friends. [Another lie] Gender doesn't matter these days. I'm pleased for him if there's someone in his life who suits him better than me.' She hoped it didn't come over as bitchy as it sounded to her.

'Is there someone else in your life, Meg?'

'Sorry, but I prefer not to comment.'

'I'll take that as a No then,' said the reporter.

'You can take it as a No or as a Yes, as you wish.'

'Can you categorically deny that there's no one in your life?'

'I can categorically say No Comment,' Meg retorted.

'What about this Lucy Plessey with whom you were arm in arm at the premiere of *As Far As the Eye Can See*? What's she to you?'

'A friend.'

'Nothing more?'

'What more should there be?' said Meg, upset at the

implication behind the reporter's question.

'Look, let's not fall out over it,' the reporter responded. 'How do you feel about being sacked by Hollywood?'

'I wasn't sacked. They didn't take up their option. Different thing.'

'Not to me. But were you disappointed?'

'Obviously.'

'Do you blame the FBI for your – shall we say? – setback in Hollywood?'

'I have no knowledge of any FBI involvement,' said Meg. A lie.

'Do you blame the FBI for putting pressure on your British studio not to offer you another picture?'

'I'm not aware that they have. I still have a contract there. It's a matter of waiting for the right picture to come along.' Although Meg knew, and the reporter must suspect, that the 'right picture' wouldn't come along.

'How do you feel about Alison Adams replacing you as the British flavour of the month in LA – a girl you helped into the business; almost your protégée?'

'I wish her nothing but the best.'

'Would your advice to Alison be to steer clear of politics if she wants to stay in work?'

Meg, riled, exposed her chin for a punch. 'If you're referring to my Vietnam campaigning, I don't regret that at all. There are more important things in life than your job.'

'Not when you're poor and have to pay the rent on Friday,' said the reporter. 'Not everyone has a trust fund to fall back on, Meg. I think we'll leave it there. Anything you want to add? No? Well, thank you. I hope our coverage will help.'

Did Meg detect a note of pity in the tough-nut

reporter's last remark?

'Who was that, darling?' Lady Chilcott asked as Meg belatedly reached the dinner table.

'Oh, just some reporter from the Daily Mirror with a couple of questions. Nothing special.'

Gradually Meg's spirits rose and her sunny view of life returned. Memories of Everard, doing this and saying that, would come at any time, anywhere, but more and more without a stabbing pain. She even found herself revisiting with enjoyment experiences they had shared. He was becoming a closed chapter, as Arnold Haverstock had before him.

And she agreed to have lunch with Roger. Once again they returned to the Old Rectory.

'Is this the only restaurant you know in Ripon?' she teased.

'No, but I believe it's the one you like best,' he replied easily.

Meg had never looked more stunning. She had abandoned her usual (figure-hugging) T-shirt and jeans for a bell-bottomed suit in lemon, with a batik shirt. Of her characteristic copper bangles there was no sign; her arms were bare. The hair cascaded as always on to the shoulders and beyond. Her complexion was clear and her eyes were large, round and bright. Roger too obviously devoured her.

But unlike last time he kept his hands and his feet to himself.

'I'm sorry about you and Everard Hughes,' he began after they sat down. He couldn't bring himself to say just 'Everard'.

'You're not sorry at all!'

'I'm sorry for you, old thing, because it's what you

wanted, but pour moi the man's a bounder.'

'That's an old-fashioned word.'

'Human behaviour doesn't change so why should the words?' said Roger sententiously. 'What else do you call a man who leads a woman on and then comes out as queer?'

'It wasn't at all like that,' Meg replied.

Roger felt the conversation getting away from him, and tried a lighter approach.

'So do I get you by default?' he asked. She recognised it as a proposal wrapped in a joke.

'You certainly have a way with words,' she joked in return. 'And no, Roger, you don't. Once and for all, you don't. I love you madly but not in that way. I'll probably live and die an old maid.'

'You're disqualified from that already, old girl.'

'You know what I mean,' said Meg.

She respected Roger for the way he handled this final ending of his hopes. No pleading, no tantrums, no walking out. In fact, they finished the meal and congratulated Monsieur Charles on one of his best efforts.

When she went into Lowmere village one morning, people whom she knew well gave her curious looks, quite unlike their usual disregard of her as just another shopper. It didn't take long to find out why. In the newsagent's her eye was drawn to the Daily Mirror. Blazoned across the front page and pointing to the coverage inside were the words THE GIRL WHO HAS NOTHING, with a picture of Meg at her bewitching best.

# Notes on the period

*Information about the Sixties appears here in the same order as the references in the story. Asterisks in the text indicate entries in this section.*

(2) AUSTIN HEALEY 3000. One of the most coveted sports cars of the period, the Healey 3000 was in production from 1959 to 1967. It was not a current model when the story opens, hence Everard's comment during the journey from Heathrow. The car is popular to the present day with enthusiasts.

(3) MICRO-MINISKIRT. The miniskirt was the late-Sixties fashion par excellence. Popularised by Mary Quant in 'Swinging London' and thence worldwide. Minis soon evolved into the micro-mini, falling above mid-thigh. The miniskirt fashion meant skimpier panties. Women were unable to control what might be glimpsed under the skirt, and so stopped worrying. Skirts became longer again, but panties continued to evolve into today's bikini-type (and externally invisible) lingerie. Another mini caught the spirit of the times – the Mini-Minor car, launched in 1959 and in production for four decades.

(5) M1 MOTORWAY. Completed from London to Leeds in 1968. The M1 was Britain's first inter-city motorway. The first motorway section was the eight-mile Preston Bypass, opened in 1958 and now part of the M6.

(6) NEW TECHNOLOGY. The now ubiquitous telephone answering facility was relatively new at this period. Pioneered commercially by Ansaphone in the United States in 1960, and the predecessor of today's voicemail from a central facility. Still in current use, the telephone answering machine has to be located with the user's telephone line or incorporated within the phone itself.

(11) RADA. Royal Academy of Dramatic Art, in London.

(13) GROSVENOR SQUARE. March 1968 protest outside the US embassy in London. The demo led to pitched battles between protesters and police, with 200 arrests.

(13) RISK BRITISH LIVES. Britain under prime minister Harold Wilson supported the US intervention in Vietnam diplomatically but declined to supply troops.

(14) B52s/AGENT ORANGE. Two of the US military's most important weapons in the Vietnam War: Boeing's B52 Stratofortress, a long-range strategic bomber; Agent Orange, a herbicide and defoliant intended to destroy the enemy's crops and forest cover. Both weapons were highly controversial because of the extensive (though unintended) effects on the civilian population. Agent Orange caused damage to human health with toxicity levels sometimes hundreds of times the safe limit.

(16) JENSEN INTERCEPTOR. Like the Austin Healey 3000, an iconic, high performance car of the period. In production 1966-76.

(20) LADY MEG DENBY. Meg as the daughter of a viscount is 'the Honourable' not 'Lady', and is addressed as 'Miss Denby'. Only the daughters of earls, marquesses and dukes are styled 'Lady'.

(29) ZERO GROWTH ECONOMY. A fashionable Sixties idea among environmentalists, concerned about the dogma of unending economic growth.

(35) MI5. The main UK internal security agency.

(39) QUEERS. The word 'gay' did not come into general use until the Seventies.

(40) JEANS. With roots in 19th century work-wear, jeans in the Sixties became ubiquitous among the young of both sexes. They were quickly popular with women for allowing the freedom of posture previously limited to men and bringing to an end former ideas of feminine deportment. For both men and women, the jeans cult spread to all ages and body shapes – often most unattractively.

(44) DONER KEBAB. Although Bob and Meg probably didn't know it, they were fortunate to find doners in Great Torrington at this time. A popular dish in Turkey, the doner kebab was introduced in England in 1966.

(46) *THE POPULATION BOMB.* Influential polemic published in 1968. The exponential growth in human numbers was highlighted in the Sixties, and has been an abiding concern ever since.

(49) THE PILL. Female hormonal contraception became available at the start of the 1960s. The Pill, as it quickly became known, was the chief driver behind the Sixties revolution in sexual attitudes and behaviour.

(61) UNSAFE IN TAXIS. A popular expression of the period.

(65) WHITER SHADE OF PALE. Procul Harum's song A Whiter Shade of Pale is an adaptation of a melody by Brahms. An anthem of the 1967 'Summer of Love', and an enduring classic. The Summer of Love saw tens of thousands of mainly young people gathering in the Haight-Ashbury neighbourhood of San Francisco for a street festival lasting throughout the summer. Hippies and various 'alternative types' were driven among other issues by anti-consumerism, opposition to the Vietnam War and a desire for peace and love. Counter-culture guru Timothy Leary uttered the famous slogan 'Turn on, tune in, drop out' at a 'Human Be-In', drawing 30,000. The Summer of Love spurred counterpart movements in major cities around the world. (See also SWINGING LONDON, p73 note.)

(65) BETTY FRIEDAN. Her book *The Feminine Mystique*, 1963, is often credited with triggering the second wave of American feminism (contrasted with earlier battles over the suffrage and legal equality issues). First president of the (US) National Organization for Women.

(66) AN MAN CHASES A GIRL until she catches him – from lyrics by Irving Berlin, 1949.

(66) WATERLOO SUNSET. Recorded by The Kinks, 1967.

(68) HE AIN'T HEAVY, HE'S MY BROTHER. Released Sep-

tember 1969 by The Hollies. The title has roots in a parable by Jesus.

(73) SWINGING LONDON. Omnibus term capturing the buoyant mood of the late Sixties expressed in fashions, music, visual arts – and a sense of transformative possibilities (see also WHITER SHADE OF PALE, p65 note). Time Magazine's famous cover of April 1966 (referred to later in the section) cemented the term in global consciousness. The writer Christopher Booker referred to the 'bewitching' character of the Sixties (although he disavowed the era).

(77) *GEORGY GIRL*. Classic Swinging London picture starring Lynn Redgrave (1966, director Silvio Narizzano).

(77) JULIE CHRISTIE. The 1965 film *Darling* also captured the feel of Swinging London. Starring Julie Christie and directed by John Schlesinger.

(77) CARNABY STREET/KING'S ROAD, CHELSEA. Twin epicentres of Swinging London in the Sixties.

(79) *BREATHLESS*. This 1960 film (original French title, *A bout de souffle*) starring Jean-Paul Belmondo and Jean Seberg, was an early and especially important example of the Nouvelle Vague (New Wave). The movement emphasised experimentation and elevated the role of the director to that of auteur (author), with figures like Francois Truffaut, Claude Chabrol, Alain Resnais and Jean-Luc Godard – who directed *A bout de souffle*.

(85) BONJOUR TRISTESSE. Song performed by Juliette Greco in director Otto Preminger's 1958 film with that title.

(86) CARRY ON SERIES. Started in 1958, the Carry On comedies eventually (1992) totalled 31 films. Although apparently low brow, crammed with double entendres and compromising situations, their high spirits and traditional British humour gave them a wider appeal, as illustrated here.

(90) CLEAN AIR ACT. 1956 act that gradually made London smogs a distant memory.

(113) J. EDGAR HOOVER. Founding director of the US Federal Bureau of Investigation, dying in post in 1972 aged 77. Hoover acquired huge power through his control of intelligence. A highly controversial figure in his later years, he specialised in targeting political activists and dissenters, and destroyed their reputations if he could.

(114) *THE FEMALE EUNUCH*. The book was not published until October 1970. Suze, with her extensive contacts in the women's movement, evidently had advance information, although she was uncertain about the author's name. Germaine Greer rapidly became an international figure and the book an important feminist text. The paradoxical title signifies the ways in which men deny women their potential.

# Acknowledgements

The author would like to thank Paul Hopkins, Margaret Hopkins, Michael Coates-Smith, Brigitte Garner and Jude Brent-Khan for their help with this book. Any mistakes of fact or judgment belong entirely to the author.

In the Notes section, information has been drawn from various sources and especially from Wikipedia. Again, any errors are the author's responsibility. Ituri Publications actively supports the not-for-profit Wikimedia Foundation, which owns the free online encyclopaedia. Wikipedia welcomes donations, small or large: **www.wikipedia.org/**

**If you liked *His Lordship's Disgraceful Daughter* please tell your friends about it! Ituri is an independent publishing house without the marketing budget of the giant corporations. (If you didn't like this novella please tell us – www.ituri.co.uk/ All messages will be answered.)**

## *When the impossible happens ...*

If you enjoyed this book, read the prequel

# Girl at the Top Table
## By Martin Horrocks

Journalist Howard Jenkins glimpses the gorgeous film star Meg Denby at a literary event, and is hit almost senseless. During the 1967 'Summer of Love', he embarks on a fevered chase in Yorkshire and London to get to know her – but how is an ordinary bloke to succeed with a girl like that?

Available from Ituri (**www.ituri.co.uk**) for £4.99, post-free within the UK, or from bookshops. (Ask us for the postage cost on foreign orders.) Girl at the Top Table is also available as an ebook from Amazon